# DON'T ASK

# FOR RULES

## A POPPY HANNAH MYSTERY

by

Jana Lynn Shellman

## Dedication

To my son, Zachary Shellman, who is the joy of my life, to my Mother, Dorothy Bristow, who this year turns 91 years of age, and to my Father James Bristow who looks out for me from the Other Side.

I also want to acknowledge all those who love me and make me content with my life as it is, dreaming of ever more.

I wish to dedicate this book to the several loyal employers I've had over the years who appreciated my skills and my knowledge, and at the same time put up with my manner of "doing things my own way."

# CHAPTER I

I can't tell you how I know, I just know. It's the same thing as when the phone rings. If the person calling is someone I'm acquainted with, then I automatically know who's on the phone before I answer it. If it's a stranger, I have no idea who's calling. I don't know how that works either. I just know if a person is guilty, I know it. If a person is innocent, I know that too. It's a gift, or a curse, depending on whether you listen to me or my boss.

I'm a paralegal and I work for Ralph Taylor, attorney at law. My favorite television program of all time was watching Perry Mason reruns, my second favorite show is Law and Order. My favorite pastime is reading case law on my coffee break. I was destined to work in the legal profession, I was born on Abraham Lincoln's birthday.

Then on top of that I've got this quirk. I can't stand an innocent person being in jail. My name is Poppy Hannah, how I got that name is another story. First I want to tell you

1

about Henry Brown.

I'd driven my Mustang convertible to the office and just had time to dry my hair. It's red. My hair, not the convertible, that's white. Naturally curly, the hair. It's a fright when it gets wet. Both the hair and the car. It had been raining for days. Convertibles are for sunny days. They don't always keep you completely dry and then this morning it wouldn't start. I looked like Bozo the clown. I spent nearly half an hour drying my hair, and trying to comb it into some semblance of normalcy so as not to frighten anyone, but what I got were two very fuzzy red pony tails sticking straight out above my ears. It was the best I could do. I was minding the front desk until our receptionist, Kara got in. She was always late. That's when Henry Brown's mother came into the office.

"I need to find my boy a lawyer."

"What did he do, Mrs. uh..."

"Brown. He didn't do nuthin'!"

"Why do you require a lawyer?"

"My boy wouldn't 'a killed nobody." For emphasis the large black woman thumped her wet umbrella on top of the monitor. A cascade of water fell down the screen, like too

2

many tears. Her aura was lavender.

"I'm sure you're right, Mrs. Brown." I brushed the umbrella gently from the top of the monitor.

"He didn't have no call to be in that neighborhood." This time the desk top received the emphasis from the umbrella.

"I can understand why you believe in him Mrs. Brown." Pulling two tissues from the box in rapid succession I wiped the rainwater tears from the monitor and the desk, once again.

"I've just gotta get him out a jail right away. He's innocent." Three rapid blows of the umbrella resounded on the side of the receptionist's desk.

"Everything will be all right. I'm sure Mr. Taylor can help you." As I gave her these reassurances, Mrs. Brown relaxed visibly. Her stern face broke into a shy smile, and she looked down as if to apologize for being so pushy. The smile fled as Mr. Taylor came rushing down the hallway like water after a dam collapse.

"What's all that knocking? Who can I help? What's going on?" Mr. Taylor is six foot one, and about two hundred pounds. He can look scary, unless you know him. He's really

3

a teddy bear.

"I was just telling Mrs. Brown that you'd be happy to represent her son at his arraignment this afternoon."

"I have a golf game this afternoon."

"It's raining. Besides, I'm rearranging our schedule. You'll still be able to tee off at 2:30, just like you planned." I indicated the schedule. He leaned over my back and looked at it.

"That's fine. But when am I supposed to eat? And when am I going to have time to shop for my wife's birthday present?"

"I'll order a sandwich," I reached under Kara's desk for my tote bag and brought out a brightly wrapped package. "and here's the gift you're giving to your wife."

"What is it?"

"It's the bracelet she was admiring at Wolfe's the other day."

"How much did it cost me?"

"You don't really want to know."

Muttering to himself he disappeared back into his office.

"He doesn't sound too excited about defending my

4

Henry."

"He's a low-key sort of guy. You've hired yourself the best lawyer in town." At the word "hired" she began to worry about money. I spent ten minutes reassuring her that it could all be arranged very comfortably, and I explained our billing system, and how much would be expected for attorney's fees if it went all the way to trial.

She left and I had to figure out what to tell the boss. He didn't believe in my powers. He just knew I was always getting him clients he didn't want to defend. He was getting to the point where he went along with me. I don't know whether he did it because he finally trusted my judgment, or whether he was trying to prove I was wrong for once.

Kara finally arrived, shaking her curly blond hair, and smoothing her tight dress over her perfect body. She described how helpless she'd felt when <u>her</u> car wouldn't start, and how five guys huddled around her engine until they solved the problem.

"Aren't men just wonderful? What would we do without them?" she gushed, as she fluttered her eyelashes. Her dark brown eyes belied her hair color, but I wasn't about to point it out to anyone. I figure you should know yourself.

5

It doesn't matter what anyone else believes to be true about you, so long as you know the truth.

I'm really not a feminist. I just believe in being independent, and honest. I don't believe any woman can be as fragile and as dependent as Kara puts on. I have to admit that she takes the dumb blond jokes really well, and basically I like her. She's a sweet girl. And really not dumb. Just kind of ditzy sometimes. And I'd be the last person in the world to hold any eccentricities against her.

I called the prosecutor's office to get a run down on the charges against Henry Brown. Fort Wayne is of medium size, once named All America City. Then a Detroit auto manufacturer opened a facility here. Since that time crime has escalated. Drug dealings and murder have mushroomed. The prosecutor's office is still struggling to catch up. They're doing a good job of it, but they're a growing family. We still call everyone by their first names.

I listened as the phone rang. I recognized my friend, Prudy's voice.

"What do you know about Henry Brown?"

"He's guilty Poppy. It's cut and dried. There was an eye witness."

"Somebody actually saw him commit murder?"

"No, but just as bad." said Prudy.

Prudy went on to fill me in. He'd been identified by an eye witness who said he'd been seen coming out of the alley minutes before the body of a small-time drug dealer was found in that same alley. Sounded cut and dried. But Henry's mom said Henry couldn't have done it, and I knew she was right. Don't ask me how. That's the hard part. I had to figure out how I knew it. I had to prove Henry was innocent.

We made a date to brown bag lunch in my office. We'd plan our Philharmonic Concert schedule when she brought a copy of the probable cause affidavit on her lunch hour. For a town of two hundred thousand, we have extraordinary cultural opportunities; the Philharmonic, the ballet, theater and four colleges, just to name a few.

"Poppy. Come into my office. I must speak to you. Immediately."

*Oh boy. Here we go.*     "What can I do for you?" I asked.

"Poppy. You've just got to stop accepting these hopeless cases. At least allow me to determine whether or not I'll take one on."

"I was sure you'd want to defend Henry."

"I don't know anything *about* Henry.  For all I know he could be an axe murderer."

"You won't disappoint his mother?"  I whined, I'm ashamed to say.

"I should let *you* disappoint his mother.  I should just put my foot down and refuse to defend him."

"That means you're going to defend him, doesn't it?"

"Lord help me.  I suppose it does...but this is the last time young lady.  Now listen to me.  None of that giggling...I mean it.  The last time..."   The bright red spikes in his aura faded into his normal calm blue.  I sighed with relief.

"Here are my notes.  I talked to Prudy.  She gave me a rundown."

"What time is the arraignment?"

## CHAPTER II

That afternoon I got to meet Henry. The boss got him out on bail. Mrs. Brown had to put her house up. They came back from Court and they went into Mr. Taylor's office. I was trying to decide whether to listen at the door or try to turn the intercom on when the boss called me on the intercom and told me to bring my pad. I grabbed it and started for the door. It occurred to me that it would be better to get everything on tape, so I grabbed a mini-tape from the desk drawer and breezed into the boss's office. I put the tape in the dictation machine and turned it on continuous play. I'm not sure he noticed. He told me to compose a quick letter to the prosecutor's office, asking for their witness list, and then he dismissed me. I left the room, sneaking a look back at the blinking red light on the machine, indicating it was still recording. I prayed it wouldn't run out of tape and set off the beeper. My boss sometimes likes to keep things from me, but how can I help prove Henry's innocent if I don't know everything?

At 2:20 I buzzed him. He had to be at the club in ten minutes.

"Maybe I can help interview Mr. Brown."

"Yeah, sure. Anything you can do," he didn't know what he was saying. He was already at the tee, even though he was only dashing out the door, searching through his coat pockets for his keys. I retrieved them from the desk where he'd dropped them this morning and dashed toward the elevator with them. I glanced out the window on the way in and saw a rainbow off to the West. God was smiling on Mr. Taylor today.

I told Kara to hold my calls, and went back to Mr. Taylor's office and sat down across from Henry Brown. The thought that I was alone in an office with a suspected murderer flitted across my mind. More quickly than that I reminded myself that Henry's Mom said he was innocent. I relaxed.

Henry Brown was a very big man. He must have been all of six and a half feet tall, and he probably weighed three hundred and fifty pounds. He didn't look like he had a lot of fat, either. He was mostly muscle. Henry Brown wouldn't

10

have had to shoot anyone. He could have picked them up and squeezed them dead. For all of that he was very graceful when he walked, and he spoke in a soft and polite manner. Besides, his aura was nearly white it was so light blue. He had a spiritual soul.

"Okay Henry. Just have faith. Fill me in. Let's start from the beginning..."

"I wasn't near that alley, ma'am. I fell asleep in my truck over on the other side of town." While he talked I removed the tape and put in a new one. I dropped the old tape into my skirt pocket.

The phone rang. "That will be your mother, Henry."

I answered the phone. It was Mrs. Brown. I assured her we had Henry right there in the office. She asked me to keep him there until she could come and claim him. Henry was thirty-five years old. Big enough to find his own way home. But if I was a mother, I'd want to keep track of my son if he was in trouble, so I agreed to keep him there until she arrived.

Before Mrs. Brown arrived, we had time to go over a lot of the points. Henry hadn't been acquainted with the man who was killed, but he knew his name. He had heard rumors

11

that the man was a small time marijuana dealer. Henry didn't think the victim was into anything more than that. Henry figured he was probably one of the little guys who dealt to the high school kids in his neighborhood. Henry didn't know a lot more since he'd been busy working, trying to get himself and his mother out of that neighborhood. Henry didn't go to the bars, and he didn't drink. He claimed never to associate with those kind of people. He was very quiet, and very shy. He shook his head from time to time, as if he wondered why, after being so careful, he still found himself in this trouble.

He swore he'd never done drugs, "My mama woulda killed me, if I'd ever got into that."

After they left I packed up my tapes and headed out the door. The phone rang.

"That's my mother, take a message." I told Kara. I knew she was calling to tell me my Avon order was in. Mom's an Avon Lady. Well, since I knew who it was and why she was calling, I struggled into my raincoat and waved at Kara as she answered the phone. I patted my skirt pocket to check on the tapes. They were still there. When I'm onto something my scalp gets tight. It was getting tighter all the time. I wish I knew why.

## CHAPTER III

It took me a little over eight minutes to get home during rush hour. One of the perks of being in the legal profession in Fort Wayne is that most law offices are clustered around the Courthouse downtown, just blocks from the older residential neighborhoods.

I was greeted by the Mouse. He's a long-haired, black, Persian/Himalayan mix with a touch of Siamese. The Siamese is just visible in the markings on his fur, a different color of black, with brownish black short-haired fur on his ears, and feet, and in his voice. He speaks Siamese-Pidgin English. His full name is Mousifur P. Tatt, and the P. stands for Puddy. After I fed him, I fixed myself a quick supper, changed into my exercise clothes and climbed onto the treadmill.

As I walked I listened to what Henry told the boss, and what he told me. The stories were nearly the same, though

13

not identical. A couple of places there were some discrepancies. That made me feel better. If Henry were lying, his stories would be identical from one time to another.

Henry was a truck driver. He claimed to have been sleeping at a truckstop on the other side of town when the murder took place. There was no one in the truck with him. He didn't go inside the truck stop, just pulled up and parked and went to sleep. When asked why he hadn't gone home, he said he was too tired. He didn't recall having seen anyone he knew, or anyone who could confirm that he'd been there. He'd slept like a log.

Suddenly I remembered I had to call my mother, the Avon Lady. Now stay with me. This probably doesn't mean anything, but the minute Henry said he'd been asleep in the cab of his truck I thought about my mother. That's when I figured out how Henry could prove he hadn't been in that alley on the other side of town sticking a knife into a small time drug dealer. All I had to do was a little leg work.

## CHAPTER IV

My Dad's hobby is citizen band radio. He loves to listen to the "traffic" on his radio. He meets people in all walks of life. He doesn't actually meet them, Mom wouldn't let him, but he talks to them over the radio. He meets truckers, farmers, housewives, hunters, bankers, preachers and even hookers.

That night I borrowed my Dad's big old Cadillac with the twin CB antennas on each fender. He calls them "beer cans". About midnight I drove across town to the truck stop, parked with a bunch of other four-wheelers and scrunched down where I could peep out over the steering wheel and keep an eye on the row of eighteen-wheelers parked across the drive. From time to time I'd hear screeching on the radio. Now and then I'd hear a trucker talking to someone on the road. Sometimes I'd hear a voice booming loud and clear. When that happened I figured the trucker was talking

15

somewhere on the lot.

It was nearly two hours later when I heard the transmission I'd been waiting for. I wrote down the information that was exchanged and about fifteen minutes later I followed a bobtail cab out of the lot and onto the freeway. As the miles crept up on the speedometer I began to wonder if I'd made a mistake and might be headed for California, but about fifteen miles out of town he put on his turn signals and pulled into a rest area. I pulled in behind him. I parked on the side with the passenger cars. From there I watched until I saw another vehicle pull into the rest area. The car parked two cars from me and a girl dressed in a short black mini dress got out and walked seductively across the grassy area to the truck I'd followed. The driver's door opened, and the driver reached down and pulled the girl into the cab of the truck. All but a tiny light at the back of the cab went out, and I could see them disappear into the sleeper, then that light was extinguished. I jumped from my car and ran down and memorized the license number on the back of the girl's car. I bought a can of pop at the concession machines, then hurried back to my car.

Suddenly I realized I was a lone female in a desolate

spot with a half dozen trucks parked nearby. I didn't know whether to feel safe or not. I got back into the car, locked the doors, popped the top on the can and took a drink. I checked the time on my cell phone and checked through contacts for the number of the police department. I punched in the number and put it back into my purse. I wanted it on the right number, just in case of trouble.

I fastened my seatbelt and put the car in gear. Somehow I had to get on the other side of the road and head back to town. I drove another five miles before I came to an interchange where I could turn around.

I got into bed at 3:30 A.M. But I was satisfied. Within a couple of hours I should have the proof that Henry was innocent.

## CHAPTER V

I was tired when I awoke at 7:00 A.M. but I had a lot of work to do. I stopped at the police station and found one of my old flames, Tommy Swift. I talked him into running the numbers on the car I'd seen last night. I fumbled my way into the office at 9:00 A.M.

"I just don't know how we're going to do Henry Brown any good," said Mr. Taylor.

"Give me a couple of hours," I replied. "I think I've found Henry an airtight alibi. The prosecutor should drop the charges as soon as they hear it."

Mr. Taylor tried to wear a look of disbelief and failed. He stalked into his office.

I wasn't nearly as confident as I sounded. I knew someone had seen Henry, but not even Henry remembered it. All I had to do was get them together. I was sure of it, because I knew Henry was innocent. His mother told me so.

19

One of my hobbies is trivia. I love to listen to stories. I retain almost everything I've ever heard. My favorite stories are those told by people who really love what they're doing. Like hunters. Hunters tell wonderful stories about hunting. Truckers tell wonderful stories about truck driving. Soldiers tell wonderful stories about soldiering. Lawyers tell wonderful lawyer stories, and you ought to hear the judge stories! If people really love what they do, whether it's their occupation or just a hobby, they tell wonderful stories. They want to share their pride with everyone. That's how I proved Henry was innocent. I remembered those stories.

Later that afternoon, the phone rang and I grabbed it before Kara could pick it up. I knew when it rang it was Tommy Swift. He had a name and address to go with the license plate number I'd given him.

I'm a twenty-three year old virgin. I'm not bragging, and I'm not complaining. I didn't plan it that way. It's just the facts. I like to do things right, and I've been too busy doing other things to do an intensive study into the subject. I want to make sure I know what I'm doing and that it's really what I want to do. I've had lots of offers for on-the-job-training, but I'm stubborn about doing it right. I've been told I'll kick myself for putting it off for so long, and that may be so, but it hasn't bothered me so far. When I see someone who really makes me change my mind, I'll let you know. Tommy was one of the guys who'd tried to change my mind. He'd come the closest of anyone, but I'd never tell him that!

"Do you know what this one does for a living?" he asked.

"Yeah, I think I do."

"Well you be real careful you don't get yourself into trouble. Guilt by association and all, you know."

"Yeah, I know. Fat chance of that. If I get in trouble I'll call you to vouch for me."

"Don't rub it in." he said. Tommy was a sweetheart. If I changed my mind, I would let him know.

Later that afternoon, with the prosecutor's promise not to charge her with prostitution, I got the driver of the car to make a statement to the police. Shortly thereafter the prosecutor called Ralph to let him know the charges against Henry had been dropped.

I got to call Henry's mother and give her the good news. She shouted out to Henry, and I swear I could hear his roar of celebration coming in both ears like stereo, he was so

21

loud!

The girl in question had been working the truck stop and had climbed up on the steps of Henry's truck after he'd gone to sleep. She'd knocked on the window of the truck. Henry'd rolled the window down. He was more than half asleep        "Do you want to party?"

"Naw, I wanna sleep." In fact he was deep in that stage of sleep called delta sleep and didn't even remember the exchange. . She identified Henry from his booking photo.

"How did you know that sort of thing went on?" asked Mr. Taylor, trying not to let on he was worried about the morals and character of his help.

I told him about my Dad's hobby, the CB set and about his handle, that's his CB name, being Rocky Rockingchair. I told him about the story my friend, BJ the trucker, told me how hookers make contact with truckers; how they go around and knock on doors and ask if anyone inside the trucks want to party. I told him about my Mom listening to my Dad's CB set one day.

About this time Mr. Taylor began to roll his eyes and get exasperated with me about not getting to the point.

That's when I told him about my Mom hearing a trucker calling on the radio for "the Avon Lady", saying he wanted to meet her out at the rest area South of town later that night to "place an order"; and about how my Mom struck up a conversation with another "Avon lady", because she thought they had something in common, and Mom let the other Avon lady have the trucker, because, "it's not my territory."

*\*\**

It was early that next weekend, a Saturday. It was still raining. I'd left the house at 6:00 a.m. I had to serve process on someone, and to preserve the element of surprise, you had to get there while they were still in their pajamas. I was already running behind, I'd forgotten the papers last night, then my car wouldn't start.

## CHAPTER VI

I rounded the corner of the fifth floor landing. Gasping, I stopped to catch my breath, leaning my hands on faded Levi's; I stared down at the wet, beat up Reeboks on my feet. The elevators were shut off for some inexplicable reason. On weekends I supplemented my paralegal paycheck by serving process on unsuspecting spouses. I had to get to my office on the eighth floor to pick up divorce papers. Flaming red hair sticking out in pony tails on each side of my head, a ragged sweatshirt, freckles and large green eyes gave the impression of innocence. It disarmed people. It was an easy matter to knock on a door, innocently inquire for the person named on the summons, hands behind my back, scuffing the toes of my running shoes on the ground. Once properly identified, I'd thrust the papers into the hands of the surprised recipient and take off running. I earned as much as $200.00 a weekend, depending on the distances I had to travel. I'd always thought it was worth the trouble, but now, panting I turned the corner to the sixth floor, the seventh floor, and I gasped for breath as I trudged up the final flight of stairs to the eighth floor, I was beginning to wonder.

"Stop right there." My heart headed for the seventeenth floor, then plummeted back down again. A clean-shaven young man held a gun on me. His hands shook so badly he had to hold on with both hands. I dropped to a step, gasping for breath.

"Okay. Put the gun down. What's going on here?"

"Did you see those cops down there?"

"I didn't see anything but millions of steps."

"Who are you? What are you doing here?"

"I'm Poppy Hannah. I work there." I pointed through the open fire door to the law office, just beyond.

"Good. Open the door and let me in."

"Why should I? Who are you?"

"Because I've got the gun. I'm the guy they're looking for."

"Who's looking for you?"

"Those cops down there."

"I didn't see any cops."

The young man sank down and put the gun on the

steps. "I don't know what I'm doing. Are you sure you didn't see any cops?" He sat on the steps and studied the toes of his boots. He was clean, and neat and didn't look like someone who was on the lam.

"Have I ever lied to you before?" I asked.

Surprised, he looked at me and gave me a slight smile. He studied my face for the first time.

"You don't look old enough to work anywhere."

"Isn't it wonderful. Thanks a lot. I work for Ralph Taylor. I've worked here for five years now. He's a criminal attorney."

"Yeah, I know. That's why I'm waiting here. I need to talk to him. The cops are looking for me. They think I killed my stepfather."

"Why would they think that?"

"He killed my mother. He got off. They said it was self-defense. I thought about doing it." He handed the gun to me. I took it. It was a tiny silver derringer. It wouldn't have done much harm. There was one bullet in it. I took it out and slipped it into the watch pocket of my jeans. He handed me five more shells. I slipped them into my pocket as well. I dangled the gun from my little finger. With the other hand I fished my keys from my rear pocket, and opened the office door.

"Come on in. Sit down. Would you like some coffee or a can of pop? There's pop in the refrigerator back there at the end of the hall." He wandered down the hall, looking tentatively into each room along the way. He stopped and peered into the library. He switched on the light and stood inspecting the books lining the walls. He turned the light off and smiled back at me.

"It smells like school in there."

I smiled. I'd always thought that, too. At that moment I knew I could trust him. He was innocent, I just knew it.

He looked into the boss's office, and then into the conference room, finally walking into the room at the end of the hall. The darkness was dissipated momentarily as he opened the door to the refrigerator and then shut it again. I heard the soft sigh of a pop can being opened. I went into my office, sat down at my desk, opened my cell phone contacts and thumbed thorough them for Ralph's home number. I've got the number memorized, but I have to check to make sure. I figure the minute I don't check I'll be wrong. To reassure the man I called out. "I'm calling my boss. You'll want to talk to him right away."

I fished the tiny derringer out of my pocket and slipped it under the envelopes in my desk drawer. I put the shells he'd given me in the paper clip tray. I'd put it in the safe with the other guns later. We have all sorts of things in our safe; guns, diamond rings, gold bracelets, titles to cars, boats, motorcycles. I call Mr. Taylor the Barter King. If it were a hundred years ago we'd have more chickens and pigs than we'd know what to do with.

"Yeah. Thanks." he said.

"How did you get into the building?" I asked as I punched the buttons on the phone. I heard it ring as he came toward me down the hall.

"I came in with the cleaning crew. I hid in the stairwell until I heard someone coming. I've been running up and down the stairs all night trying to keep out of sight. I saw lights on in here. I thought there was someone here who could help me. It was just the cleaning crew, apparently. I need a lawyer. I met a trucker who recommended your boss. I found his address in the yellow pages. I called, but nobody answered. I couldn't stay home, so I was going to stay downstairs in my car. Then I saw the lights on up here, so I came up."

"Do you know the trucker's name?"

"No, he was just a really happy black man. He said Ralph Taylor was the best lawyer in town, but I knew the name from the papers, too. He helped get that ranger guy off who was accused of killing those campers. I followed that. It always seemed wrong to me. I've always thought of rangers as good guys."

"That's what I told Ralph, too. He didn't want to take that one. He thought the guy was guilty. I wouldn't let him give up. I just knew a ranger couldn't be guilty."

"Is that a good reason to defend someone?"

"It's not a logical reason, I suppose, but it was mine."

"You mean your boss didn't think the guy was innocent?"

"Not until I found the evidence of poaching being done in the State Park. It was winter. Nobody was supposed to be in the park except the ranger and those campers. Nobody had checked through the entrance but them. It made sense to the police when they arrested him. It didn't make sense to me. How many crooks do you know who register their presence? Well, anyway. That's what got me checking into things, and I finally figured it out."

"Do you think your boss will believe me?"

"I don't know. Probably not. But that doesn't mean he can't help you." I replaced the receiver on the phone. "He's not answering. He might have unplugged the phones. He does that sometimes, so I can't find him."

"Now what do we do?"

"Why don't you tell me why the police think you killed your stepfather."

"I threatened to kill him. I don't feel sorry that he's dead. He killed my mother. He claimed it was self-defense. They let him go. They didn't even have an inquest, just let him go."

"Why didn't they have an inquest?"

"'Cause he was the town marshal and he had everybody snowed. They all believed him."

"Do you know anyone else who could have killed him?"

"Almost anyone. He was a tyrant. Nobody liked him that well. He went around like a sheriff out of the old west, wearing six-guns and a cowboy hat."

"I think I read about that in the paper."

31

"He was always pushing someone around. The thing is..."

"What?"

"I was considering doing it. I thought about killing him. I even went out and bought a rifle with a night scope, so I could get him. I just couldn't get up the nerve to do it. I even stalked him one night. Stood over in the willow stand across from the house. Followed him all over town, had him in my sights more than once."

"What stopped you?"

"I kept hearing my mom's voice in my head, telling me not to let him drag me down to his level. She told me that when I had my first argument with him. She said he couldn't help being the way he was and to just let it go. She said I shouldn't let it eat at me. I should get on with my life. That's when I moved out and went on my own. That's what did it. I just kept hearing her voice saying, 'Danny, he can't hurt you if you don't let him.' I just couldn't do it."

"And the police found your weapons?"

"Yeah. It almost looks like somebody's been looking over my shoulder. He was shot at night. I'd just bought the night laser scope. He was shot with a Remington 30.'06. I'd just bought one. They found brass from Winchester 30.'06 ammunition on the ground near where the shots were fired. I had three boxes of Winchester 180 grain 30.'06 ammunition in my room. They found prints in the mud where they think the shots were fired. They've identified them as being from Nike high tops. I have Nike's too. Everything points to me. The only thing, my shoes were clean. They'll just claim I washed them."

"It makes you look pretty guilty, doesn't it?"

"Yeah. Almost as if I really did it. If I didn't know better, I'd believe all the evidence."

"How did you know they were looking for you?"

"They searched my room. I'd been staying out West of town with a friend. He tracked me down at a girl's house. Told me the cops had come and taken my stuff away with them. Said they were looking for me. He told them he didn't know where I was. He really didn't. He just knows some of the places I hang out."

"So why didn't you turn yourself in?"

"Like I said. I'd believe I was guilty, if I didn't know otherwise. But I didn't do it."

"I know you didn't. Everything's going to be just fine.

Now...what are we going to do about it?"

Answering my own questions, I continued..."I'll run out to Ralph's house. I still have to serve these papers. No one will be in the office to bother you. Why don't you go in the library and stretch out on the couch and take a nap. We've got a cable hookup on the tv in there. Make yourself at home. I'll serve these papers, get Ralph, and then come back. Everything's going to be all right."

He visibly relaxed when I said everything would be all right. I guess he believed me. He looked as if all of the air went out of him, though. He was so tired he didn't even answer me. He held up one hand. I followed him to the library and switched on a small table lamp that cast shadows into the corners. There weren't any windows. It's a perfect place to take a nap on a rainy day. I found an old blanket and pillow I keep for my own office naps, and he took them and made himself a nest on the couch. I left him there to get my papers.

I grabbed my umbrella and purse and started for the door. I thought of something I wanted to ask him and went back to the library.

"By the way, Danny...what's your last name?"

He was sound asleep. I clicked off the table lamp and crept out of the room.

I locked the office door behind me. No one was scheduled to be there until Monday morning. He'd be safe. I ran down the stairs, whirling around the corner post at each landing. It's easier going down than coming up. The only person in sight was the weekend guard, half asleep in the lobby.

"You sure do work hard," he said.

"It only looks that way," I saluted him as I went through the revolving doors onto the street.

## CHAPTER VII

"Not another one! Where do you come up with these losers?" shouted Ralph.

"I've never brought you losers!" I protested truthfully.

Not one of the cases I'd brought to him had ever been a loser. He'd won them all. Every single case I'd pressed him to take had turned out to be a winner, because none of them were guilty. I just always know.

"What's his name?"

"I forget. I think it's Denny or something."

"So what makes you think Whatzizname is innocent this time?"

"He thought the library smelled like school."

"Aaaagh!" Ralph sat down on the steps of his porch and removed the muddy loafers he'd been wearing in the garden. His hair was wet and the clothes he was wearing were soaked clear through.

37

"What have you been doing?"

"I've been pulling weeds."

"In the rain?"

"They come out easier when it's raining."

Ralph had his own idiosyncrasies. That might be why he'd always been so tolerant of mine. But it wasn't in his character to let me off easy. He always had to make a big deal out of my strange quirks.

He placed the muddy loafers on the back porch and motioned for me to follow him into the kitchen. His wife, Ruth, was stirring soup on the stove. She always looked like a television mom, wearing a cotton dress and an apron. I'd never seen her in blue jeans or shorts. The table was occupied by Ralph's three children. They were arranged like stair steps. There were two empty places at the table. Ruth quickly set out another placemat and without asking ladled a bowl of soup and placed it at the extra chair she pulled from the desk.

"You'll eat with us," she announced taking my purse and papers and pushing me down into the extra seat. I didn't mind. The soup smelled wonderful and I was hungry.

"It doesn't have a face," said Elizabeth, the four-year-old.

I'm a vegetarian, and don't eat anything that has a face. The children know that.

"No. It is pure vegetable soup. No meat." said Ruth.

"Poppy has found me a new client." said Ralph, "She thinks he's innocent."

"Of course he is," said Ruth, "Poppy always knows."

"Always knows." said two-year-old Teddy.

"Poppy knows everything." said Elizabeth her brown pony-tail bobbing as she nodded her head.

"Poppy can do anything," said seven-year-old Julia, the serious one.

I just love visiting this family. It makes me feel so warm, so loved, so competent!

The boss glared at me. I scrunched down behind Teddy in his high chair.

"Knows." said Teddy as he stuck an upside-down spoon into his ear. I took the spoon from him and dipped it into his soup. I blew on the soup. I looked up to see Ruth shaking her head vigorously. It was too late. Teddy blew the soup out of the spoon and grinned triumphantly at his feat of strength. I wiped the soup from my face and arms.

"Why don't you love Poppy, father?" asked Elizabeth.

"Love Poppy." said Teddy.

"I pay Poppy. That should be enough." He finished his soup, hugged Ruth and patted the three children on the head.

I ducked as he reached out to pat my head.

He grabbed his briefcase. I quickly slurped up a couple of spoons of soup, thanked Ruth and followed him out the door.

He got in the passenger side of my car. I put the key in the ignition and turned it. Nothing happened...except for the strange noise Ralph made. He jumped out of the car, marched through the rain to his garage and backed his car out. He threw the hood of my car up violently, wrenched a pair of battery cables out of his back seat and attached them to my car battery, and then to his own battery. I turned the key again and the car started instantly. Ralph glared at me the entire time he backed his vehicle into the garage.

Ralph and Ruth live in a upper middle class addition not yet annexed into the city. Ralph is torn between fighting annexation, and becoming a resident of the city so that he can be named to one of the mayor's committees. That's a

40

Libra for you.      He  continued  to glare until we were halfway to town.  Then, as I drove he turned and looked into the back seat.  "What is this, a rolling garbage can?"  Then he questioned me.  "What makes you think this person isn't guilty?"

"I told you.  He thinks the library smells like school."

"You must have a better reason than that."

"Well you remember the story about his stepfather shooting his mother?  He claimed it was self-defense, but at the time she was shot, Danny's mother was talking on the phone to her daughter."

"So?"

"So.   How could that be life-threatening to the stepfather?  Can you see someone talking on the phone to someone, pulling a gun and shooting someone at the same time?"

"Maybe she hung up the phone."

"The daughter heard the gunshot that killed the mother."

"How do we know it wasn't the gunshot the mother fired at the stepfather?"

"Because there was only one gun, his.  And only one

shot fired from it. The one that killed the mother."

"We don't have to prosecute the stepfather. He's dead. We have to defend the stepson. He had a terrific motive for killing him."

I drove on, deep in thought. I had to figure that part out. He hadn't broached the subject of how Danny was going to pay his attorney's fees.

Ralph the mind reader asked, "And how's this guy going to pay his fee? Have you talked about fees with him?"

"That will work itself out later, don't worry about it. Everything's going to be all right." I said.

***

Later that afternoon Mr. Taylor met with Danny and Danny agreed to turn himself in that evening so he could be released on bail the next morning.

## CHAPTER VIII

As I walked in the door of the office Monday morning, Kara began gesturing frantically to me to take the phone call away from her. She put the caller on hold, and I picked it up again.

"Is there any way I can help you? I'm Mr. Taylor's legal assistant."

"This is Harold Rivers. I'm Gerald's brother, Danny's uncle. I just know Danny couldn't have killed Gerald. I wanted to let you know I'd cover Danny's legal fees. Pull out all the stops. I've wired $15,000. You should be getting it any time."

"Mr. Rivers. I'm sure we'll be able to get along just fine with that for awhile. Thank you."

Harold Rivers went on to say that he lived in Arlington, Virginia, and worked in Washington, D.C. for the Drug Enforcement Agency.

"If you need any kinds of lab tests or the like, give me a call. I can get them done quick."

"We'll keep that in mind. Do you have any idea who might have wanted to kill Gerald?"

"Well, I've got to admit, I've wanted to kill him a time or two. It would be easier to make a list of those who didn't want to kill him. Nevertheless, he's my brother..."

I promised to keep in touch with him and let him know the progress we were making. He gave me several numbers where he could be reached, including his car phone.

It was only later and too late to ask him how he'd learned that we were representing Danny. We hadn't even filed an appearance yet.

***

Ralph came back from Court with the bad news that Danny hadn't been brought in for arraignment, and would have to spend the night in jail. They lost his paperwork and didn't get him processed in time for the morning hearing.

44

## CHAPTER IX

As soon as I got off work and got the battery jumped again, I headed for Fairview, twenty miles West of town. I'd been there a couple of times before for a Fall Festival, and in high school I'd gone there for music contest. It hadn't changed much in the past five years. In fact, it probably hadn't changed much in the past thirty years.

Entering town you crossed a bridge over a river, which was most likely the reason the town was originally placed there. The main street was dissected by swinging a stop light. There was a five and dime, a drugstore, a couple of antique stores, two or three tiny restaurants, a barber shop, three gas stations, and three taverns. Standing at the stoplight you could see the residential district fitted onto the ends of the business district like green bookends, where the trees and yards started. If you turned around three hundred sixty degrees where you stood, you could see church spires

45

sticking up above the trees in every direction. I counted five as I turned. Crossing the railroad tracks you'd come upon the tall grain elevators, and just beyond were the farms, and you were out of town. It felt as if you could blink, and all of the cars disappear and you'd see wagons being pulled down the street by horses; and if you stood by the bridge you could imagine Indians trading with the settlers.

Maybe I'd been there before in another life. It felt like a good place to be.

I had the top down, daydreaming about being an Indian maiden drifting down the river in my birch bark canoe, when a blast from a semi-tractor brought me back to the twentieth century. It was a wonderful summer day, the scents of the river and the nearby farms wafting on the warm breeze, but the blast on the horn was enough to remind me there had been two murders in this idyllic little town in the last six months.

I read off the list of people I wanted to talk with to the man at the filling station. He pointed to a good-looking man across the street. I left the car and waved as I crossed.

The first person I'd found was Gerry Rivers, aka Gerald Rivers, Jr. He was standing beside a gold 941

Porsche. I assumed it was his.

"Hi. I'M Jerry with a G." His handsome face broke into a friendly grin.

"I'm working for Danny Johnson's attorney."

"Oh, that's great. I mean, Danny's my brother. I'll do anything I can to help."

As he stepped nearer to me, I caught a whiff of expensive cologne. It definitely made standing closer enjoyable. Unfortunately, the information he had to give me wasn't much help. We both prolonged the conversation and started talking about other things. He seemed incredibly upset about Danny's problems, and appeared to be searching his mind for anything that could help me prove Danny innocent. He was movie-star handsome, with dark hair, a terrific tan, and the most gorgeous eyes I'd ever seen. He had the physique of a body-builder. As we stood talking, I noticed girls walking by, giving me a killer-look, and looking at him with longing. He didn't seem to notice them at all. He was very attentive, almost too attentive, for no longer than we'd known one another, but I have to admit that I was flattered by the attention. He asked for my telephone number and suggested we see one another. I didn't say no.

He gave me permission to look over the scene of the killings, his father's house. He wasn't living there anymore. The state police were through with their investigation.

"The tape outlining the position of Dad's body is still on the floor of the porch. I only went back to get the stuff I needed. It's been locked up since he died." He handed me the key. "There's nothing left to find, but be my guest."

I wished he'd been able to give me some more information about his father, about Danny's involvement in the family, or something that would give me a lead. I realized that he hadn't been terribly helpful in my investigation. I also realized that I'd failed to mention that his Uncle Harold had stepped in to pay Danny's legal fees. Of course, I had forgotten to mention that to Ralph as well.

The fact was he'd not seemed free to talk about the murders, but neither did anyone else in town. Everywhere I went I got scared looks, or anger.

"The killer is still loose," the waitress at the small restaurant said. But she wouldn't elaborate. And neither would anyone else.

"The murders are just the tip of the iceberg," said the bartender at the Talking Parrot bar.

"There's more going on here than anyone wants to admit, and it ain't just in Fairview either...goes all the way back to Washington, D.C.," said a man who was sitting at the bar. He wouldn't give me his name. He wouldn't elaborate.

The Rivers' house was within walking distance, like everything else in town. It was a beautiful day, and I enjoyed the walk. The smell of honeysuckle and summer flowers permeated the air. As I walked beneath the full green trees, the soft breeze touched my cheeks. The less welcome scent of sun-dried grass and dirt filled my nostrils as I took a shortcut over a vacant lot, and the touch on my cheeks turned to a dry, hot rasp. I stood on the front porch and looked toward what I thought was the grove of willows across the street where Danny believed the killer had hidden to shoot Gerald.

The front porch was screened in all the way around and the door to the porch wasn't locked. A swing was hung to the left of the door into the house. I went and sat on it, and looked at the outline on the floor. It appeared that Gerald was just entering the main part of the house when he was shot. There was a spray of blood on the side of the door. There was a hole in the screen where the slug had passed

49

through on its way to Gerald. I got up, rubbing the slat marks off the backs of my thighs, and tried to look out the bullet hole with my back to where Gerald's outline lay. I couldn't reach it. I looked around and found a small wicker footstool. I stood on that, the wicker creaking and complaining about my weight. I had to bend my knees to put my eye to the hole. If I turned with my back toward Gerald's outline, I was looking across the vacant lot, not at the stand of willow trees.

I pulled the screen door open, stepped down from the porch, and the door flapped shut behind me, barely grazing my ankle as it did so. I walked across the street to the vacant lot.

There was an alley at the back of the lot, and just this side of the alley was a large dumpster. I wondered how long it had been there. I walked behind the dumpster and looked toward the house.

I had to climb up onto the dumpster to see over it. There was a ledge that ran along the side where the carrier truck slid its arms in to pick up the container. When I stood on that, I could see Gerald's porch, and I could see the swing through the screen.

I walked around the dumpster once again. The ground

looked very hard and dry. There were thin tire tracks in the hardened mud next to the container, like a garden tractor or motorcycle. There were some pointy toed footprints in the mud as well.

I took pictures of the prints in the mud, and made some notes with my cell as I walked back to the house. I looked over toward the willow trees. If you were going to shoot someone from there, you surely wouldn't wait until your victim was about to enter the house to do it. The shot wouldn't clear. You'd almost have to do a bank shot!

I took some more pictures with my cell phone, and then I sat down on the swing again and made a quick sketch of the porch, the position of Gerald's body, showing the willow stand, and the dumpster across the street. I thought about the peace and tranquility of swinging on a front porch in a small town, the sounds of birds singing, squirrels chattering, jays shrieking, and the warm soft breeze coming through the screens, the ever-present scent of honeysuckle. How much safer and content could one feel. I sighed and looked back at the yellow tape outline by the front door.

I returned to my drawing. I couldn't make it to scale, but tried to show the approximate distance and angle by guessing. I made a note to ask Danny why he thought the killer had hidden in the willow stand.

Gingerly stepping around the yellow tape outline of Gerald's body, I entered the house with Gerry's key. I was instantly assaulted by the odors of a refrigerator left too long without care, and a garbage can that hadn't been emptied. Flies buzzed between a storm window and its double hung partner. The scent of stale tobacco filled the air as well. It was an ordinary looking house, cluttered with stacks of things. From the front door you could see into the kitchen to your right, a dryer stood open, and towels and sheets spilled out onto its door. The sun streaming in the windows filtered through the dust I'd stirred as I'd entered. A table was positioned so that one could sit and look out the front window onto the porch. A single plate with dried food stuck to it was on the table together with a half-full cup with dried coffee sticking to the bottom. The closer I got to the kitchen the more unpleasant the odor coming from the refrigerator, which still hummed.

It was obvious that there hadn't been a woman in the house for several months prior to Gerald's death. But it was also clear that there had been a woman's influence in the decor. There were objects on the tables and the walls such as one would purchase at home interior parties. The cupboard had its share of Tupperware containers. A dead spider plant hung above the kitchen sink.

I searched what must have been Gerald and Alice's bedroom. It smelled of stale tobacco and a fainter smell of sachet, which grew stronger as I pulled open the top drawer of the dresser. It was empty. A locked gun cabinet held a number of rifles, including a 30.06. On the unlocked shelf above the cabinet were boxes of various sized shells. I pulled open a drawer in the bottom of the cabinet, and found five pistols including a .357 Magnum and a black powder pistol assembled from a kit. There were also bullet dies in the drawer. I found a reloading device in the closet. A large box on the floor of the closet was stuffed full of women's clothes. Men's clothing occupied the hangers in the closet, but were all shoved to one side, as if awaiting another closet partner. Empty hangers cascaded down the side of the dresser, linked together in a waterfall. The bed was unmade. The room held a stale, sweaty smell. Half of the drawers in the chest of drawers were empty. The left hand side of the dresser was empty. In the bottom drawer of the right side I found a stack of pornographic magazines. Under them I found a legal envelope bearing the return address of a Washington, D. C. law firm. I tucked it under my arm. It wouldn't hurt to borrow it.

There were only three rooms and a bathroom downstairs. The bathroom smelled damp and musty. Soap had dried on the bottom of the tub, and there was a deep rust stain in the stool. Someone had removed the tank lid and failed to replace it securely. The police had probably looked inside. I lifted it. There was a lot of rust. On closer inspection, I could see that something square had been placed up against the one side below the water level. It had left an outline. There were two thin black lines at the top of the tank. I looked on the floor, and found a hanger bent into shape of approximately the same size, with two hooks that could have gone over the lip of the tank. I tried it for size. It fit exactly. I tucked the hanger into my bag of tricks.

I threaded my way up the steps through stacks of clothing, and stacks of women's magazines and copies of Guns and Ammo to a large room that occupied the entire second floor. The room smelled musty, as if it had a leaky roof. It was separated by the stairs, and appeared to have been Gerry and Danny's room.   On a night stand next to a double bed on one side I found stacks of mail with Danny's name.   Half of it wasn't opened and was dated before his mother's murder.   There were shelves on the wall above the bed filled with a diverse selection of books, from <u>Zen and the Art of Motorcycle Maintenance</u>, to <u>The Complete Works of Shakespeare.</u>   There were also books on guns, basketball, and a number of biographies, including Abraham Lincoln, Marilyn Monroe, John Lennon and Martin Luther King.   A copy of Playboy magazine lay on the bed.   The dresser next to the bed was empty.

The other bed was a single bed, and there were bows and quivers full of arrows slung on the wall behind it.   There was a picture of a high school girl stuck in the mirror over the dresser.   A  picture of a young Gerry between a couple, presumably his mother and Gerald was propped up with a bottle of Brut.   A dimestore mirror, a black comb, some change, a pack of Marlboro's, a cheap lighter and a package of razor blades lay on the nightstand next to Gerry's bed.   A rolled up business card lay on the floor next to the bed.   I picked it up and straightened it out.   It had the name of a used car dealer in Collington.

I went back to the kitchen, noting the position of the telephone, and that it had a relatively short cord. I rummaged in the drawers until I found some plastic bags, then went back around the house retrieving items of interest. Apparently the police hadn't found them interesting, but I did. It's that trivia thing again.

I locked the house and looked back. It was a pleasant looking house.

Not many neighbors were home in the Rivers' neighborhood. I found one, Helen Lawrence, who knew who'd lived in the Rivers house back to the time it was built in 1903. She knew Alice when she was a little girl, and knew Alice's parents. She was a gold mine of information, or misinformation. I wasn't sure which.

Her hearing was good, and her eyesight was better. She credited her habit of walking everywhere she wanted to go with her good health.

She claimed to have heard the argument and the gun shot that killed Alice.

"Gerald was screaming at someone, then I heard Gerry yell something, then I saw Gerry go down the street toward town. Then about five minutes later, I heard Alice scream, 'You can't fool me, I know you', and then I heard the gunshot."

"Did you tell the state police that?"

"The state police never asked me if I heard anything."

"Did you testify at the inquest?"

"Nobody asked me to testify. I'm not even sure they had one. I thought sure I'd hear from someone, but nobody asked if I'd heard nothing 'til you."

She was awakened by the gunshot that killed Gerald. She said she heard a "lawnmower" across the street in the vacant lot just after the gun shot that killed Gerald.

"Gerry and Danny were both nice boys. They mowed my lawn for me. Alice took me to the grocery store every week in the winter."

No one had asked her if she'd heard anything when Gerald was killed either.

"Do you think that the shots fired came from the willow stand across the street?"

"Why no, they came from behind that dumpster over there. It made a funny echo, like the gun had been on top of the thing. You could hear somebody jump down off it, then I heard that lawnmower start up."

I checked around with other neighbors, and they either didn't have anything to say, or didn't want to talk to me. One man told me it wasn't healthy to ask too many questions about it. Another man said, "I'm not risking my life by talking about anything."

## CHAPTER X

I'd left the car sitting at a filling station, just in case... It didn't start. While the man rolled a battery charger out and hooked it up to my car, I got myself a Coke from the machine. Sugar and all. There was a disreputable-looking gentleman leaning against the machine. His clothes were brown, his face was brown, his shoes were brown. Dirt brown. Even his grey hair was dirt brown. He had to move so I could get the can out of the machine. He wobbled and lurched toward the door frame, where he positioned himself very carefully so that he could look at me. It was only by his movement that I could tell he was still alive. The stench would have led me to believe he had died.

"The killer is still loose," he said. He chuckled when I started. He stepped closer.

I looked at him again and retreated from the odor.

"I've heard that," I said.

"Nobody will ever guess."

59

"Could you tell me?"

"Nope. Mebbe later," he slurred as he waved a dirty paper bag wrapped tightly around a small bottle. He lurched and shuffled his way toward the side of the building where he disappeared. His aroma lingered on.

His aura was even dark brown. I'll have to ask Hazel what that means. Hazel, my housekeeper knows what the colors mean in auras.


I went to interview Alice and Gerald Rivers' neighbor, Mildred Newell, she'd lived to the West of the Rivers up until the week of Gerald's murder. Now she had a little cottage overlooking the river on the outskirts of town. Alice was big through the chest, and had strong arms and strong legs sticking out from a worn cotton dress. She looked as if she could wrestle a hog, yet she behaved in a ladylike manner, being sure to keep her knees together when she sat, then bustling about picking up magazines and stacking them, as if she was ashamed her house wasn't better kept.

"I just couldn't stand to look at that house no more. I was afraid to go to sleep at night, thinking about the violence there. I couldn't stand it no more."

I wanted to ask her how the family got along with one another. She told me that Gerald and his son, Gerry had moved to town when Gerry was fourteen. Mildred stood up, tugged her cotton print dress down over her hips, and patted her bosom. She straightened the knick-knacks on the table, and used the hem of her dress to dust here and there as she talked.

"Gerald's always been weird, as long as I've known him."

"What do you call weird?"

"He had one of them there short wave radio sets up in his attic, and I'd hear him up there all night long sometimes talking out loud. I don't know whether he was talking to himself or to the radio. Sometimes I'd hear a lot of static, and sometimes I'd hear voices kind of tinny like. I guess it was the radio."

"Did he ever talk about his hobby?"

"You know that's what's funny about it. I said just that. 'How's your hobby coming along?' You know, trying to strike up a conversation, and he said 'I ain't got no hobbies.' Then after that he put up a roller shade over the window. But in the summer he'd have the window open and I could still hear him talking, and I could still hear that tinny sound."

"Is that the only weird thing he did?" I asked, making a note to ask about the short wave radio. There hadn't been one when I was in there, and there wasn't an attic.

"That's just the tip of the iceberg! He was okay when he first got here, but just after he married Alice, he started dressing up like a sheriff out of the old west, with cowboy boots, a cowboy hat, and guns in holsters," she said. "Then next thing you know he'd be acting like a big city police detective in a dark suit for awhile before he'd go back to his cowboy suit. I always wondered if he wasn't one of them schizophrenics."

"You mean someone with a split personality?"

"Yeah, one of those schizophrenic persons." she repeated. I didn't bother to explain schizophrenia.

"How'd he dress when he interviewed?"

"When he first appeared before the town board to be hired, he looked real ordinary. He was wearing a dark suit and a tie. He seemed real normal."

"What kind of credentials did he present to the board, do you know?"

"All I can recall is that he said he'd been working for

the Washington, D.C. police department, and he wanted to get his kid out of the city because there was too much crime and violence there," she cocked her head and then snorted.

"Looks like he brought some of it with him, doesn't it." I said.

"Yeah, kind of ironic, isn't it?" she asked.

***

I went to interview the Town Clerk, Karen Arnold. I wanted her to tell me how long Gerald Rivers had been the Town Marshal, and how the town came to hire him. Karen, slightly built with glasses perched on the end of her nose, seemed torn between telling me everything she knew and getting on with the pile of invoices she had in front of her. She finally pushed aside one pile, and picked up another and began folding them and inserting them in envelopes.

"I've got to get these water bills out, or there won't be enough money coming in for my paycheck."

"Was Gerald Rivers paid by the town as well?"

"Don't get me wrong. There's always enough money to pay everyone, it's just that it never looks like we're going to make it another month. It's gotten better lately."

"Why?"

"I don't know.  Maybe we got ahead, we didn't have a town marshal for awhile, and we didn't have to pay anyone. We have a deputy marshal.  That was Everett Meadows and he's acting town marshal now.  He's getting paid the same as he was before.  Still..."

I waited for her to continue her thought.

"It seems like we're doing better now than we were there for awhile."

"Has there ever been an audit?"

She gave me a shocked look, and stopped folding invoices.  She pushed herself away from the desk and went around behind a larger desk six feet away from where I was sitting.

"Are you saying that I've been dishonest?"

"Good heavens, No.   Let's look at this another way. Is there any way anyone could get their hands on town funds without going through you?"

"Well, they're not supposed to, but I suppose it could be done."  She suddenly looked thoughtful, pulled out a desk drawer and began leafing through a ledger.  Several minutes passed, as she pulled out a large checkbook, and placed it above the ledger.  She had forgotten that I was there.  I

64

cleared my throat. She jumped, then pulled a brown sweater up over her shoulders.

"Oh. I'm sorry. Forgive me. I get sidetracked sometimes. Do you have any more questions? I'd like to get this work done." I excused myself and left her, her hands running nervously through her hair as she leafed through a ledger, looking for something. I had an idea there might be an audit.

I interviewed Donald Strahm, a member of the Town Board to check into Gerald Rivers' credentials for the job of Town Marshal. Mr. Strahm had an insurance agency located in an office on the main street of town. The office was sparsely furnished, with two desks, two desk chairs, and two side chairs. A computer sat on the receptionist's desk. The receptionist was very young, dressed in a mini-skirt, cracking gum rapidly, as her fingers flew over the chattering keyboard, entering data. Her employer had discarded his suit jacket and loosened his tie.

As I entered the door, I saw one of his shoes scoot out from under the desk, appearing not to be occupied by a foot. Suddenly Mr. Strahm became shorter as he slid down in his chair in an attempt to retrieve his shoe. The receptionist distracted me by asking my name. By the time I'd supplied it, and she'd written it on a slip of paper, Mr. Strahm was standing and walking toward the front desk, hand outstretched, both shoes on his feet.

"Hello, I'm Don Strahm, can I help you with your insurance needs?"

He appeared crestfallen when I told him my purpose in being there, but he recovered quickly, and offered me the chair next to his desk, as well as a cup of coffee, and a cigarette. I declined the last two offers, and asked him how long Rivers had been town marshal.

"He came here the first year I was on the board. I didn't have much experience with running the town then, and pretty much relied on the older members of the board for that decision."

"Do you regret the decision to hire Gerald Rivers?" I asked.

"Sometimes it seemed like a bad idea, especially when I learned of the things they say happened back East."

"Back East?"

"His first wife, or maybe it was his second wife was murdered. He claimed he came home and found her dead.

66

I understand the murder has never been solved."

"Was he a suspect?"

"I guess he was, but there was never any evidence that placed him there at the time of the murder. He and his son claimed to have been touring museums on the mall in Washington, D.C. And then there was his brother-in-law."

I had to feed him another question. He seemed reluctant to speak ill of the dead. "What about his brother-in-law?"

"His wife's brother, was shot outside his apartment in Georgetown, just about a week before Gerald's wife was killed."

"Was Gerald a suspect in the shooting?"

"Again, he claimed to be someplace with Gerry. I don't know how his alibi stood up, but nobody ever connected him with that killing either. I didn't really start to wonder about it all until after Alice was shot."

"Did you know all of these things before you hired him?"

"We knew his wife had died, but we didn't know the circumstances. I think the sympathy vote, you know, widower with teenage child living in a dangerous city like Washington,

D. C., I think that's what made us hire him. I've always regretted that decision. I worry someone will hold me responsible for that decision. Yes. I regret we hired him. I wish I could do it over again. Yes."

"Have you learned anything more about him since his death?"

"I asked around his old neighborhood and the police department in Washington. Took the kids there for a visit last April to see the Cherry Trees and to go through all the museums. There weren't a lot of people that knew him, but there was one neighbor who seemed to think there was some mystery. He didn't say Gerald killed his wife, and his brother-in-law, but he thought Gerald's actions had something to do with it. He implied Gerald was a crooked cop."

He went on, "I learned the Washington, D. C. police department were following some lead that had to do with his job, and a Colombian drug lord. It seemed Gerald had accidentally made an arrest of a courier who was carrying close to a million dollars worth of cocaine in the trunk of his car, which ultimately led to shutting down a multi-million dollar drug business. Gerald was never involved past the initial arrest, but the police department had a couple of reasons to think these people were behind the deaths. That's why Gerald went into hiding by coming here."

"Why was the brother-in-law killed?"

"I don't know. My information was Gerald and his family had just moved from that apartment building. They lived with the brother-in-law. A case of mistaken identity was the cops answer."

"What about the wife?"

"I guess they figured she was killed because they couldn't find Gerald. It doesn't add up, and they seemed not to have any more answers. I told them about the deaths here, about Alice and Gerald. They didn't seem anxious to follow up."

After fending off questions about my life insurance needs, I decided to head back to town. As I was pulling out of the filling station once again, a White Cadillac pulled out in front of me. I had to jam on my brakes to keep from hitting it. It raced off down the road. I left town in the opposite direction and thought no more about it.

*****

"What in the ... ?" I turned my head sharply and looked behind me. That stupid so and so just rammed right

69

into the back of my car!    The road was narrow, just wide enough for two cars to pass if you weren't on a curve.

"How do I get away from this maniac?"  Jamming my foot onto the accelerator I sped away only to see the white Cadillac keeping pace with me,  though there was more space between our cars.  The road is wet, I can't go too fast.

"What in the hell does he want? He's driving like he's trying to kill me."  The white monster hit my rear bumper again.

"That's it.  He's trying to kill me." I tried to go faster, but he kept up with me.  I squirmed uncomfortably as sweat ran down the center of my back.

"Why would he want to kill me." I kept glancing in the rearview mirror hoping to catch a glimpse of the driver, but all I could see was the glare of the headlights coming closer again.  I fumbled in my purse trying to find my cell phone.  I picked it out of the mess and it flipped out of my hand onto the floor as the white Cadillac slammed into the back of my car again.

## CHAPTER XI

"Did you see that? He tried to nudge me off the road!" Have you noticed I'm talking to myself? Well, I do that all the time. You'll note I even answer myself. It helps me get things in perspective. You'll also note I make inappropriate comments, as if I'm not afraid. Don't let it fool you. It's my reaction to being scared. I figure I have a choice between joking or screaming hysterically. Since I'm a control freak, I opt for jokes. It doesn't stop the cold fear from racing down my spine. It doesn't stop the bitter taste I get in my mouth, and it doesn't keep my legs from growing weak.

"Maybe if I jam on the brakes he'll go around me." I followed my own suggestion. My car fishtailed to a stop, the rearend had slid into the ditch. The big car just missed hitting my front fender as it streaked past me. I got my breathing back under control, then backed up and headed back the way I'd come. In the rearview mirror I could see the bigger

71

Cadillac had stopped and was turning to follow me. I pulled into a driveway and began honking the horn. The bad driver in the white car sped on by, back towards Fairview.

"Well, you dummy. When you had the chance you should have gotten the license number!"

"Maybe you'll get another chance." Sure enough, I saw the lights coming up behind me. Maybe it was someone in a hurry to get to the big city. No. I could see the outline of the car in the rearview mirror. It was him.

We were just at the outskirts of the city, when the Cadillac passed me so fast, he nearly took my doors off. There was no license plate. He disappeared down the street and around a corner. Hopefully I was through with him.

I adjusted the rearview mirror and proceeded cautiously down the dark street, my heart jumping everytime I saw headlights coming in my direction.

It was raining lightly. The storm's arrival had been announced by tremendous winds. The rain was almost a disappointment. The way the storm had blown in, I'd expected trees to be lying in the road. Instead the wind had gone, leaves scattered about as if someone had dumped their lawn trimmings. A paper fluttered softly at the curb, not yet glued to the street by dampness. My headlights cast shiny golden streaks in the wet asphalt. From time to time a silvery moon of light reflected down from a lamp post. There was little traffic.

I relaxed my shoulders and settled down in the seat. I shook out my left leg. It had been jammed into the firewall behind the pedals. A little uptight, Ms. Hannah?

A squad car pulled out of a side street just ahead of me. With a sigh of relief I followed it to the center of town, where the traffic picked up, noting as usual the storm seemed to have veered away from the center of town and the three rivers that converge there. Indian myth has it the three rivers coming together keep tornadoes from hitting the city. Later new age theory says the three rivers coming together create an electro-magnetic vortex that heightens psychic phenomena.

Still no white Cadillac. Hopefully, I was through with this adventure.

I headed for home. A bit more wary, and a lot less frightened. But smart. I backed into my driveway and shut off the lights. I felt around on the floor for my cell phone, then I got the key ready and put my purse strap over my shoulder, opened the car door and raced for my front porch. There was a sudden burst of sound when Marge's dog began barking. My heart settled back into its proper place as I fitted the key into the lock.

I entered quickly, locking the door behind me. I flipped the kitchen light on and was hit full in the chest.

## CHAPTER XII

I picked the furry black mass off my chest, claws withdrawn, but hissing furiously. I hadn't fed my cat for nearly twelve hours. He was really upset with me. His name is Mousifur P. Tatt. The P. stands for "Puddy".

There was a note from Hazel on the refrigerator. "Be sure to take your vitamins. Remember even vegetarians need protein." The dishes were done, everything sparkled. Good ole Hazel.

I poured myself a glass of juice, and went through the mail she'd left on the counter. Bills and junk mail. No one ever writes to me.

The land line rang. I picked it up with excitement, and answered seductively, "Hello, there. Long time no see." The only answer I got was a click and a dial tone. Either he chickened out, or my powers are slipping and it wasn't who I thought it was.

75

It was midnight when I turned off the lights and climbed into bed. I usually put myself to sleep with subliminal tapes to cure me of my weaknesses, but tonight I wanted my ears unencumbered. I heard every sound inside and outside the house, until I finally drifted off. The last thing I remember is the Mousie, lying on my knees, kneading the blanket with his paws. At least he was on watch. I slept soundly.

## CHAPTER XIII

The sunshine gave a sparkle to the world, still damp from the rain. The air smelled heavenly. As I surveyed the kitchen before pulling the door shut and locking it, I saw the black furry monster purring contentedly from the top of the counter. I'd remembered to feed him and myself this morning. It looked like it was going to be a great day.

When I arrived in the office I set about fixing Ralph his coffee. I don't drink coffee, but he does. He says I make surprisingly good coffee considering. I don't know what he's considering when he says that.

I gave Kara work to do, and she was busy answering the phone and taking messages. I'd gone through the stack of mail by the time Ralph came in. He'd just been to Court. He brought back the bad news that Danny had been denied release on bail. The Prosecutor argued that with his mother dead and no other living relatives in Fairview, he'd be likely to

77

run.

I gave Ralph all of the arguments I thought he should have used to override the prosecutor, and he informed me that he'd used them all himself without my reminding him. I thought it would be a good idea to change the subject. I didn't really mean to tell him about my adventure, it just slipped out in the normal course of conversation.

"How's Ruthie and the kids?" I asked.

"They're great. How are you?"

"I'm fine. Oh. By the way, I went to Fairview last night to see if anyone knew anything?" My voice ended in a question, fishing for approval.

"Did you learn anything?"

"No. Except someone is trying to get me to stop asking questions."

"What makes you think that?" Kara was standing behind Ralph, curiously listening as well.

"A big white Cadillac tried to force me off the road on the way home."

"That's it! You're through with your investigating. Now. I mean it! You've got to stop before you get yourself hurt. If you don't stop...I'll....I'll....I'll....Fire You!" Ralph was turning red in the face. Kara scooted back to her desk before he could turn on her.

"Elizabeth would never speak to you again."

"I know. But you've got to stop stirring things up. Let the police do the investigating. Let me do the lawyering. You do the research and the typing  and all the other things you do so wonderfully."   He stalked toward his office.

"Thank you.  Sure.  Okay." I tried to sound meek. He turned back toward me.

"Just PLEASE don't do anything to get hurt. If you got hurt, Elizabeth would never speak to me again."

"Can I get off a little early?  I want to go talk to Danny." Kara had just started back into my office.

"Don't you ever listen to me!?  Please!" He shouted. I caught a glimpse of Kara's back as she snuck back down the hallway to the receptionist area.

"Well, I suppose I can wait until 5:00." I said.

Ralph glowered at me, then turned his back and started toward his desk. He growled and turned back toward me with a slightly less ferocious demeanor than before.

"I'm going to talk to Danny this morning.  If you have anything to ask him, I'll ask for you.  Just stay out of it, now.

Do you hear me?"

I sat down and began typing, nodding my head, hoping he would take that as agreement. It's hard to type with your fingers crossed. I didn't want to hurt Ralph's feelings, but he needs me to check into things. So does Danny. I can't help myself. I do try to stop short of practicing law or interfering with a police officer in the line of duty, but darn it, if I can do something to help, then I just have to do it!

## CHAPTER XIV

Ever since the bar association made paralegals associate members, I'd had a bar card that got me into the jail on business. It helped a lot now. For a town that's geographically about the same size as Paris, but with two and a half million less people, we've got a pretty big jail. Drugs. Murder, burglary, robbery, prostitution. Most felonies appear to be as a result of the drug business. There are fewer murders in Paris than there are in Fort Wayne. It's scary.

Danny looked much younger and much more frightened as he was led down the hall, his hands cuffed in front of him, with matching Sheriff Deputy bookends. I smiled at him as they entered the visitor's area. He smiled and gulped.

"Could we have some privacy here?" I asked as they positioned themselves at the end of the table.

"You sure?" asked one deputy.

81

"I'm fine.  Just give us some space."  They withdrew to just outside the door.

"You doing okay?"

Danny crossed his arms on his chest and looked at me.  "I don't think I'd better tell you anything more."

"Why not?"

"I don't want you getting hurt on my account."

"I didn't get hurt.  Nobody else is finding anything that will help you.  I'm all you've got right now."

"Yeah.  Well....but you'd better be careful.  I heard about your close call."

"Never mind.  I didn't get hurt."

"You could have.  Weren't you scared?"

"No.  Yes.  But nothing happened.  I'm okay now."

"Just take it easy, okay?"

"Do you mind if I tape this?   I need to know why you bought the kind of rifle you did."

He gave me the same look Ralph had given me this morning, shook his head, took the tape machine from me and pushed Play.  "I don't know.  When Mom first married Rivers, Gerry and I used his dad's 30.06.  I guess it was just familiar."

"Do you know if his dad still had his rifle?"

"Sure. It was in the gun cabinet at the house the day Mom was killed."

"How can you be sure?"

"I wondered what he'd shot her with. I looked in the gun cabinet."

"What did he shoot her with?"

"He used the .357 Magnum he carried in a shoulder holster."

"Who knew that you bought the 30.06 after your mother was killed?"

"Norm sold it to me. I guess he could have told anyone. I didn't. I took it home and hid it in the closet."

"Because you were planning on using it on your stepfather at that time?"

"Yeah. I guess I was pretty ashamed of myself. I didn't go anywhere or do anything. Just sat around thinking about what I thought I had to do."

"What did you do with the gun after you decided not to kill him?"

"I just threw it in the back of the closet."

"When was the last time you saw it there?"

"The day I threw it in there. I tried to get out and see

friends and quit thinking about it after that. I wasn't home much of the time."

"How can you explain the rifling on the slug matching your rifle?" I asked.

Danny shrugged. "I can't."

"Where were you the night he was killed?"

"I was up at Rochester at a bar until 9:00 o'clock. Then I just drove around. About 2:00 A.M. I went to my buddy's. We had a couple of beers and talked until 3:00. I left to go home, but I was pretty soused. I couldn't keep my eyes open, so I went to sleep in my car. I didn't figure I'd oughta drive."

"Do you know what time he was shot?"

"Five A.M."

"Where were you parked?"

"About two blocks away."

"What an alibi! You could have done it, and pretended you were asleep in your car. You could have gotten there and shot him and gotten back right away."

"Anybody could have gotten there and gotten back right away. We're talking about Fairview here." Danny looked disappointed. He turned around in his seat as if to escape. One of the deputies opened the door and came in. I motioned for him to go back out. Danny turned back toward me, and said, "I thought you believed in me."

"I do believe in you. But listen to what I'm saying, and then think about it. It's what the prosecution is going to say."

Danny shrugged and relaxed. I was doodling, trying to come up with some answers.

"What time did you wake up?"

"I might have woke up earlier, I can't remember. But I think it was about 5:30 or 6:00 when I really woke up. I heard sirens. There was a lot of traffic down by Rivers' house."

"Did you go down there?"

"No. I couldn't bring myself to go back down there after the night in the willow stand."

"Did you see anything unusual? Anything out of place?"

"No. The only thing I saw was old lady Duggin walking her dog."

"Did you see any cars or trucks?"

"Nah. Just a guy on a motorcycle."

"What did he look like?"

"Just your normal biker. Black leather jacket, jeans, black helmet."

"Had you ever seen him before?"

"I don't know. He had on a full-face helmet. I didn't recognize the bike. I think he was just riding through."

Danny didn't have much more to say about the killing, and about his motives for considering the murder of his step-father.      I started to leave, then turned and asked him to tell me about Gerry.

"We were good friends for a long time. After Mom died he stopped talking to me. I guess he felt guilty because he knew his dad had killed her, and he knew it wasn't right."

"What kind of a person is he, Danny?"

"He's okay. Like I said, used to be a good friend. We'd get together and put down his old man for being such a jerk."

"How was he a jerk?"

"Oh, he was always calling him, Gerry the Fairy."

"Is Gerry gay?"

"Nah, I don't think so. It was just his old man's way of getting to him. He was always calling him a sissy. I think he was trying to get him to fit his image of what a man should be, which wasn't all that great."

"What kind of image."

"The Marlboro Man, a cowboy, a hero, all those fake things that don't mean anything.  Gerald would dress up like a cowboy, thinkin' it made him look like the Marlboro Man."

"How would Gerry react?"

"He'd just leave.  He wouldn't ever fight.  That would just make his old man that much madder.  He thought it proved Gerry was a sissy."

"I talked to Gerry yesterday.  He asked me out."

"Yeah?  I'd ask you out, if I were out!"

"Well, until we get you out, what do you think?  Should I go out with him?"

"Yeah, sure.  I don't know why not.  He doesn't date a lot.  Can't remember the last time he went out with a girl.  But he's okay.  Maybe not your type, but he's okay."

"What makes you think you know my type?"

"He tends to be pushy.  He cultivates a bad boy image. He tends to hang out with some low-life types.  I didn't think you'd dig that kind of thing."

"You're right, I guess.  Except almost all women are attracted by the bad boy image.  I'm not sure it's a healthy attraction, but it happens."

"Maybe that's my problem. Maybe this thing will improve my reputation." He smiled.    I got up to go. He grabbed my hand. The deputy at the door, looked worried and started into the room. I waved him off. I like someone holding my hand.

"Be careful. I meant it about asking you out if I get out."

"Not if...when," I said.

He smiled.

## CHAPTER XV

"Start you rattle-trap! Start!" Shouting did no good. Nothing is more disgusting than a car that won't start. My friendly neighbor, Marge, waved from her window. Seconds later she emerged from her front door carrying a set of jumper cables in one hand and waving her keys in the other. This had become a routine over the past week. I was going to miss seeing Marge every morning once I got the old bomb fixed. Several minutes later my car was purring and chattering.

I hugged Marge, slammed down the hood, threw her jumper cables in the backseat, said, "I wish someone would steal this darn thing and fix it for me," and headed for work. As usual I had to detour around street repair. This will be a nice town when they get it finished, but they never finish their "civic improvement."

Once I got to the office, I spent a lot of time on the phone, exhausting minor leads. I had to limit my phone calls. Ralph was keeping an eye on me. Kara was covering for me. I had her taking messages from certain people so he wouldn't suspect I was talking to them. He was much more vigilant than usual. Ruth must have read him the riot act, because of the incident with the white Cadillac. He kept me busy writing a brief that didn't need to be done for a month. He usually waited until the night before it had to be done and expected me to write fifty pages or more in a couple of hours. I knew the brief would be altered substantially before he was through with it, so I just typed it on the computer and ran it off in between my phone calls. He left the office at 4:40. There was a message for me from a name I didn't recognize. I called it.

It wasn't until a man's voice whispered hello, and I'd asked for the name on the message that I recognized the name. It was "Earl S. Gardner". At least that was the way the name was spelled on the message. (Kara isn't a reader.) The person who came on the line was very rude, very adamant and very much to the point.

"Stay out of this, or you won't see Christmas."

I asked, "Who is this?"

"Donald Lam," he said.

I doubted that. Donald Lam was the name of one of Erle Stanley Gardner's fictional investigators.

He went on to outline the various things that would happen to me, if I didn't stop "nosing around." I know it was supposed to scare me, but that's one of the weird things about me. I don't like to let anyone know I'm scared. It embarasses me. And then I get mad because I'm embarassed. It's rare I'll cry because I'm scared. I may have been scared, but I was also mad, and I couldn't wait to get back to the hunt. Someone was afraid I was finding out way too much. Once I got past the scary part, it excited me. I was on to something. My scalp tightened. I felt as if I were wearing a hat.

I left the office at 4:45. I told Kara I was going to the courthouse. She winked at me as I went out. I collared a legal secretary, Penny, on the elevator and conned her into coming with me to give my car a jump start. Marge's jumper cables were still in my car.

It took me seven minutes to drive from the center of town to the city limits, and only because I just missed rush hour.    One of the perks of living in this town is its quick exits to the countryside and to the lake.

Lake is a misleading term.  If someone says "I'm going to the lake." You have to be sure to ask, "which lake?" if you care, because there are hundreds of lakes.  If they tell you Long Lake, you have to ask whether it's Upper or Lower Long and in what county.  Many lakes have the same names.

I got to Fairview about 5:25.  I asked around and found the old inebriated gentleman I'd talked to on my last visit was known as Shorty.  I learned he was the town's only Harvard graduate, and he had a degree from Harvard Law School.  I was told he hung out at the Talking Parrot, a small bar on the main street.  I found him there occupying a stool at the bar. A couple of other men were strung out along the bar. Everyone seemed to be drinking alone.

Someone had gotten to him.  He didn't want to talk. The two men at the bar finished their drinks and left.  Shorty moved closer.  He had an aroma of stale cigarettes, spilled beer, and that peculiar perfume of age.  I endured this assault on my nostrils. The excited glint in his dark eyes was a strong attraction.

"The killer is still loose," he said, taking another swig

from his glass of beer, draining it.

"Do you have any idea who the killer might be?" I asked.

He shook his head and held out his glass.

I must have looked puzzled. What does an empty glass have to do with anything? Then I remembered my detective stories. Shorty must have remembered, too. Information always costs something in those stories.

I motioned for the bartender to pour Shorty another beer. Instead of asking if I wanted anything, he asked to see my identification! I wonder if they'll ever believe I'm over twenty-one! I started to ask for a glass of water, but thought I'd ought to order something I could pay for, since I was occupying a stool. I ordered a cup of coffee. As I watched the bartender pouring it into a cup I was thankful that I didn't actually drink coffee. It looked too thick to pour, and too thin to plow.

Shorty sipped his beer. I swear he was purring.

"Do you know any more about this?" I asked.

"Try to find one of them Hell's Angels."

""Hell's Angels in Fairview?" I was astonished. "Can you give me any more information?"

93

"Nope."

"Do you know anyone else who might know something?"

"Annie." He drained the beer. He held the empty glass toward me. I motioned the bartender to refill it.

"This is the last one he should have," said the bartender.

"Do you have any ideas about who might have seen something the morning the town marshal was murdered?"

"Like he said. Annie might know." said the bartender.

"Who's Annie?"

"Annie Duggin. She's sort of our resident Bag Lady."

"Where can I find her?"

"She has a house back in Brooklyn."

"Brooklyn?"

"Actually Brooklyn Street, but it's on the other side of the tracks. It's like a separate little town back there. Shacks and run-down houses. A couple of people live in an old bus back there, and there's one place used to be a railroad car. Shorty can show you where she lives."

"Yep." Shorty offered. He slid down from the bar stool, downed the beer, wiped his mouth on the sleeve of his

94

worn brown wool suit coat and shuffled out the door. I followed him, running to catch up.

"Can we walk from here?"

"Always do."

I breathed a sigh of relief. I'd parked my recalcitrant vehicle at the same filling station as before. This time I'd asked the man there to put a battery charger on it, first thing. I didn't relish the idea of having Shorty's special scent with me in the car for weeks to come.

We arrived back in Brooklyn and found Annie's house. I'd expected something trashy, but her house was a cute little cottage with a white picket fence and flowers. Annie, however, wasn't nearly as neat as her house would lead you to expect. She appeared to be wearing all of the clothes she owned at one time. She could have been a gypsy. Her head was wrapped in a babushka, and she was wearing at least one dress, a sweater and an apron. When she smiled, you wondered at her chubbiness. Only two teeth were visible. How could she eat?

Shorty introduced me as a private eye. It impressed Annie so I didn't correct him.

"Do you have any idea who shot the town marshal?"

95

"Nope.  Didn't do no harm, though."

"What do you mean?  It <u>killed</u> him!"

"Didn't do nobody else no harm."

"Didn't you like him?"

"Didn't nobody like him."

"Was there anyone, specifically, who might have wanted to kill him?"

"It'd be easier to say who wouldn't a wanted to kill him."

"Why didn't you like him?"

"He was always telling me to stay off the street.  He never said it to me, but he told me Shorty was an eyesore.  Said he made the town look bad.  I figured when he told me to stay off the street he was telling me the same thing."

"That wasn't very nice."

"He killed her, you know."

"Who?"

"Gerald.  He killed his wife.  For no good reason."

"They said it was self-defense."

"She wouldn't have hurt nobody.  She was a real lady."

"Do you think Danny killed him?"

"Nope.  Think you should find the man on the

96

motorcycle."

"What did he look like?"

"Had on one of those black helmets that covers the face. Wore black jacket and blue jeans."

"Where did you see him."

"He roared away from the marshal's house that morning."

"Where were you?"

"Me and Shorty were in the alley behind the restaurant, looking for throw-aways."

"Had you ever seen this man on the motorcycle before?"

"Don't know. Never saw the motorcycle before. Shorty called it a hog."

"It was a Harley. A hog," said Shorty.

"Do you have a dog?" I asked.

"Yep, Priscilla there." As she said the dog's name, it suddenly appeared. She pointed to a mutt, with an amalgamation of ancestoral ties, fastened to the side of the house. "She helps us find the good throwaways."

I found my way back to the filling station, climbed into the car, turned the key in the ignition and was greeted by the familiar rumble, purr, clatter, I'd grown used to prior to the balky battery problem.

As I drove out of Fairview, I kept my eyes open for that white Cadillac. I thought about the mysterious motorcycle rider. Danny had mentioned him, and now Annie had mentioned him. It shouldn't be too hard to learn who he was. The drive home was uneventful. I rolled down all of my windows, and drove leisurely back to the city. I glanced in my rearview window from time to time, half expecting to see a monster vehicle bearing down on me. The monster never showed.

I backed into my driveway. Marge waved to me from her kitchen window. The light was fading. I was hungry. So was the black furry monster.

I was just turning out the lights when there was a knock at the front door. Thinking it was Hazel, I pulled the front door open. I knew as soon as I did it, I shouldn't have. Two men pushed their way inside waving semi-automatic pistols.

# CHAPTER XVI

They were both wearing ski masks. One was slight, and only a little taller than me. He had effeminate mannerisms, and almost seemed to fear the gun he was holding in his hand. His gloved hand was shaking. As he passed close to me I caught a whiff of one of my favorite perfumes. He was wearing Georgio.

The other was much larger, and much more scary. He grabbed me by one of my pony tails, and whirled me around, shoving me into an overstuffed chair in the living room.

"Where is it?" the big one asked. He didn't wait for an answer, but began ripping drawers out and strewing the contents all over the room.

"Oh, great. Now I'm going to have to call Hazel." I said.

"Who's Hazel?" he asked.

99

"My housekeeper. You don't think I'm going to clean up this mess, do you?"

The smaller one held a gun on me, while the big one ransacked my house.

Only the big one talked. He kept yelling things at me, and asking me where "it" was. I didn't have the slightest idea what it was, and I told him so.

The small one hit me up side of the head with the butt of the pistol. The blow wasn't enough to knock me out, but it knocked me down and made me mad. Just as I was about to retaliate, the big one came back into the room. He pulled me to my feet. Mousie had jumped to the top of the bookcase by the door. The big guy turned his back to the door, motioned for his partner to leave, and was just about ready to turn and leave himself when he turned back and ripped the living room phone from the wall. At the same instant Mousie launched himself from the top shelf onto the big guy's face. I saw the claws go through the ski mask, and the man let out a screech. With both hands he shoved the cat away from him.

I was afraid he was going to shoot the Mouse. I picked up a chair and threw it at him. He went flying out the door and off the porch. I ran to the kitchen to the phone. I should have run out the door to see what they were driving. Instead I called Tommy. In my present state of fright, I was about to ask him to spend the night.

## CHAPTER XVII

It was two-thirty in the afternoon. It had been a long boring day. I'd needed that after the harrowing experiences of the night before. Tommy had shown up with another officer on the force, and we filled out an incident report. There was actually no proof of the fright I'd had, except for the phone being pulled out of the wall, stuff strewn all over my house, and the obvious agitation of the Black Furball. He didn't even want Tommy to have anything to do with me, and he loved Tommy. A crime technician came out and managed to extract some skin from beneath Mousie's claws. It probably wouldn't amount to anything, but it was a clue. I'd managed to stop shaking and was not hyperventilating by the time Tommy arrived, so I didn't bother to ask him to spend the night. We won't tell him how close he came to an invitation, it would probably depress him.

Any way, after all that, I welcomed the dreariness of

the following work day.

I tried to keep the news about my night visitors from Ralph, but it only took one trip to the Courthouse for him to learn of it. He came back in a real frenzy, ranting and raving about my safety and how Elizabeth was really going to kill him, and he fired me once or twice. Kara cowered in the hallway, then beat a hasty retreat to the ladies room. His answer to the whole thing was to give me idiot labor to occupy my time. First there'd been an estate accounting to work on, and second, Ralph insisted I help Kara file the past week's correspondence. Ralph knows that, in order, those are my two least favorite jobs. I love searching for information to go into the accounting, and I love looking through the files for information, and I love doing research and writing. But I always procrastinate about accounting and filing, which tends to make the jobs bigger than they need to be. Besides the filing is supposed to be Kara's job.

I finished the estate accounting, and complimented Kara on the wonderful way she had with the filing. I told her I never know where anything is, and I wouldn't know what to do without her. It's the truth. I hate filing.

Prudy called and talked for awhile, and Hazel called to

remind me to eat. I called the man who repairs my car, and he said it would be next week before he could get me in for a tune up.

The girl who'd jump-started my car last night wasn't around, but I found a stranger in the parking lot who was accommodating, and I was soon on my way to see Danny's sister, Evelyn Cray.

Evelyn was a surgical nurse, and she had married a surgeon. They lived in one of the beautiful old mansions on Old Mill Road, surrounded by oak trees, with acres of lawn. I pulled into the circular drive, up to the front door, and got out, leaving the engine running.

Evelyn looked a lot like Danny, the same coloring, and the high cheekbones. Danny's eyebrows grew together in the middle. I suspected that Evelyn had plucked hers to keep them from doing the same. The big boned look didn't flatter her as well as it did Danny, but she was a very handsome and attractive woman. Her hair was cropped short, but it was so thick that you didn't feel as if anything was missing. She still seemed to be all female. She was comfortably dressed in a draped peach blouse, and peach slacks. She had gold sandals on her feet. She wore no jewelry.

Danny had told me that she'd married and moved away from Fairview ten years ago, when she was twenty. They'd become successful in a number of ways, all generating tons of money, and she'd talked her husband into moving back to be nearer her mother and Danny. She was older than Danny, and now her mother was gone, she felt as if she had to replace her mother in Danny's eyes. She regretted she hadn't done a better job of it, and she believed Danny had probably killed Gerald. Danny knew her pretty well, because this is substantially what he'd told me about her. Her sister Victoria now lived in California. It was to her sister her mother was talking on the phone when, according to Evelyn, "Gerald murdered her in cold blood."

"Do you remember where you were when Gerald was shot?"

"Are you asking me if I killed him?!"

"Don't worry, I ask everyone that."

"Well, I was in the Bahamas with my husband when it happened. We came back as soon as we heard they were looking for Danny."

"How did you hear?"

"My housekeeper sent me a wire."

"Do you know anyone else who might have done it?"

"It could have been half of Fairview. Everyone hated him."

"That's what I've been hearing." I thanked her for her time, and left. The gas tank wasn't too much lower than when I'd left it, but I stopped on the way home to fill it up.

I backed into the driveway. Mousie greeted me at the door.

"There's got to be some brown rice in here someplace." I muttered at the contents of the refrigerator. "All of these containers. There has to be something real to eat in here." I found the brown rice. The date on the lid was just two days ago. I dumped it into a pan, grabbed a half-full container of salsa and dumped it into the rice. I found a match and lit the stove. The rice began to sizzle, I turned it down. I located an open bag of tortilla chips and sat down at the table to munch until the rice was hot.

I'm a terrible housekeeper. I can get it done if I set my mind to it, but most of the time I forget. That's where Hazel comes in. I hired her because her name was Hazel. My grandmother was a wonderful housekeeper and her name was Hazel. Then there was that old black and white sit-com about the housekeeper with the same name. Except for being a bit nosy and her more youthful appearance, my Hazel lived up to her namesakes. She's a good housekeeper. She comes in an hour every day and keeps my place in order. She takes care of everything. It amazes me she can work one hour and do a job it takes me a full eight hour day to do if I try to do it myself. And she's got other talents, too. Most importantly, she's sort of psychic like me. I mean, we're not witches or anything. It's just she knows things ahead of time, like I know who's on the phone. She's pretty good at it. It's called precognition. The only thing is, when she tells me something, I'm never sure if it's from her conscious knowledge or whether it's something "they" told her. Sometimes she doesn't know either. It makes it hard to figure out what to take seriously.

I write notes to myself and put them on the refrigerator door. Hazel's been known to take it upon herself to help me out if she sees a note that interests her. For instance, the night after Danny showed up in the office, which was a Saturday, I put a note on the fridge that said "Go to library, look up Danny Johnson -- Alice Johnson Rivers killing, -- Gerald Rivers killing." I hadn't gotten around to it. Hazel had.

On the table were a stack of photocopies of the newspaper reports of each killing. At the bottom of the stack was a note from Hazel, written in her large, loopy handwriting. Paperclipped neatly to that was a bill for photocopying. The note said, "my friend Ethel tells me Danny was a great newspaper carrier, never missed a day, his teachers say he got good grades, Rev. Watson says he recommended him for law enforcement. He didn't kill Rivers. He'd planned to, but gave it up." Now how did she know that? I know I didn't tell her what Danny had said to me at the jail.

I rescued the rice from the stove just as it started to scorch. I dumped it into a bowl and piled shredded lettuce on top. I pulled a jug of herbal tea from the refrigerator and poured a glass. A sip told me it'd been in there too long, it was beginning to taste stale. I absently spooned rice and chips into my mouth as I read the newspaper accounts of the killings. Like Danny'd said, he sounded guilty.

Dialing the phone, I peeled a banana. I rummaged in the freezer and found a carton containing a couple tablespoons of vanilla yogurt. I dumped it into a bowl, and listened to the busy signal. I pushed re-dial and sliced the banana onto the frozen yogurt. From a paper carton on the counter I dipped natural, freshly ground peanut butter onto the top. The busy signal buzzed back at me, so I hung up and dipped a spoon into the glop I'd just created. I rolled the mixture around on my tongue until it melted. Suddenly the phone rang. It was Ralph. I picked up the phone and cradled it so as not to interfere with the rest of my dessert.

"Hello Ralph."

"Will you stop doing that!" he screamed.

I held the phone away from my ear, "Stop doing what?"

"Saying 'Hello Ralph' before you know it's me."

"I don't say it before I know. I know it's you when it rings."

"How do you kn... Never mind. I called to tell you someone tried to kill Danny. They've taken him to the hospital. He's under guard. He was stabbed in the side when he went to work out in the gym. I've got an order for him to be held in isolation as soon as they return him to jail."

## CHAPTER XVIII

"Why would someone want to kill him?"

"Maybe they're mad at him for killing Rivers."

"Maybe they killed Rivers and think killing Danny would put an end to the investigation. Maybe Danny knows who did it, but just doesn't know he knows."

"Don't you ever give up? You could be wrong. He could be guilty."

"Can Elizabeth hear you?"

"Yes. She's sitting here shaking her head. Okay, Elizabeth, I know. Poppy knows everything."

"Not everything. I don't know who killed Rivers and I don't know who tried to kill Danny, but I'll bet they're connected. I've got to talk to a couple of friends. I'll get back to you."

"Stay out of trouble. Don't be taking chances. My wife would kill me if you got hurt. So would my kids."

111

"It almost sounds like you care."

I don't want a lot of static at home, okay?"

As I hung up, I could still hear Elizabeth in the background chanting, "Poppy always knows, Poppy knows."

I finished my vegetarian meal and rinsed the dishes in the sink. On the refrigerator was a chart, courtesy of Hazel listing the food groups and what a vegetarian has to eat to get all her vitamins. So far I was about five days behind Hazel's schedule.

I called Tommy Swift and grilled him on what he'd heard about the stabbing in the jail.

"I don't know too much about it. Heard it was a druggie who just got arrested today. Said it was his mission."

"Do you know who arrested him?"

"I can find out for you. What do you need to know?" he asked.

"Just find out for me how serious the charges were, and if we've got any clue to who he's working for," I said.

"You think this guy got himself arrested just so he could do Danny?"

"I've heard of stranger things."

"Is this one of your psychic clues?"

"How can you separate the psychic clues from your own hunches?" I asked.

"You've got a point."

He made another plea for a date, and I replayed in my mind the times we'd gone out, and how sweet he was. But right after that I replayed the part about how he wanted me to marry him, and settle down, and stay at home all the time, so I politely turned him down with a promise. "You'll be the first to know if I change my mind."

I'd just hung up the phone when it rang again.

"Meet me at the feed mill," the strange voice whispered into my ear, "at midnight." It frightened me. Before I'd picked up the phone I'd been sure I'd known who was calling me. I was surprised when I didn't hear the voice I expected. It must have been wishful thinking or something.

## CHAPTER XIX

"Come to the feed mill at midnight. I have proof that Danny didn't kill his father." The voice had whispered to me through the telephone lines.

Danny Johnson was laying in the hospital under police guard and nobody believed he was innocent ... except me, Ruth, Elizabeth, Julia and Teddy. They believed it because I said so. I had to check it out. I'm not totally stupid, though. I thought I'd better not go unarmed. I'm not crazy about guns, and I don't like having to carry them around. Ralph has had fits whenever he's found out about it. But one of my best friends is a retired police officer, and she has given me very good safety instruction, as well as good pointers on what to look out for when you're on the street. Not all knowledge is dangerous. Unless you listen to Ralph.

I stopped at the office. The cleaning crew was gone, and all the lights were out. Fortunately the elevator was

115

working. The lights were still on in the hallway. I let myself in. Glancing through the waiting room window I saw the silhouettes of the high-rise bank buildings downtown, each new building competing to be the tallest in town. I stepped closer to the window and looked down. The tall buildings created a tunnel, generating winds that didn't exist five blocks away.

The downtown lights cast a silvery glow on the inside of the office. The light wall colors picked up the outside lights and reflected it. It was still spooky. I turned on the lights and went into the copy room. The refrigerator hummed as I twirled the dials on the safe. The door popped open. The stale air fell out. I opened another door inside, and gingerly picked over the pistols there. I selected a .9 mm Biretta. I knew how to load it and how to use it. I set my purse on the floor and rummaged through the safe for a clip and box of shells I'd put in the bottom. I loaded the pistol clip and emptied the rest of the rounds of ammunition into my jacket pocket. I put the gun in my purse, slammed the door of the safe and turned to leave. I turned back and twirled the dial. Ralph had fits if he found the dial pointing to one of the numbers of the combination.

I turned off the lights, and checked to make sure the door was locked. When I pushed a button for the elevator both of them arrived. I call the North elevator alternately Darth-vator or Demon Drop. I chose the South one, which I have affectionately christened Ellie-vator. I looked both ways before I opened the lobby door, and with keys at the ready raced toward my car, which I'd been able to leave right in front of the door with the top down. It's hard to lie in wait in a car with the top down, and now I had my gun. I felt safe, but visible.

I was soon on my way to Fairview. I'd taken a chance, carrying the loaded pistol in my purse. I had a permit, but I didn't have it with me. It might even have expired. I couldn't remember. Something I ought to leave myself a note about later.

It looked like it might rain. From time to time I saw flashes of lightening far off to the West. As I entered Fairview, I noticed the stars and the moon had disappeared. The street lights cast wavering shadows as the wind shook the tall posts. No one was on the street. As I crossed the railroad tracks at the far end of Fairview, I observed a small light in the office of the feed mill.

## CHAPTER XX

Suddenly the entire sky lit with the fury and intensity of a million thunderstorms.  It wasn't a thunderstorm, it was a fire storm.  A huge blast of fire was lighting up the area in front of me where just moments before I'd seen a tiny light in the feed mill office.  In the light from the fireball I could see the force of the explosions throwing grain silos high into the air.  The strength of the blast threw me across the front seat of my car.  The car rocked back and forth, then settled.  My side ached.  I'd bruised my ribs on the passenger arm rest.  Suddenly a hail of grain descended on me.  As the hail storm of grain and debris settled, through the dust I could see nothing.  Had someone been waiting in the office to give me proof of Danny's innocence?  Or had someone been waiting to blow me up because I was getting too close to proving it myself?

Suddenly the sky was lit behind me by real lightening,

and the wind picked up, and great gusts blew from the West. The fire in front of me blazed higher. The counterfeit storm before me was being challenged by nature behind me. As the wind became more furious, I heard the wires overhead begin to sing. The trees shook violently as the wind became more ferocious. The fire blazed even brighter in front of me.

Sirens roused me and I turned my car around, to head back toward the city. I pulled into an alley, turned off my lights and held my hands up in front of my eyes. My hands were shaking. I carefully slowed my breathing, then, as rain drops began to fall, I raised the convertible top, snapping it in place. Volunteer fire department cars raced toward the burning feed mill. My whole body was shaking as I climbed back into the car and eased it onto the street and headed for the highway out of town.

The thunderstorm had tamed itself down to a steady patter as the storm clouds raced ahead of me toward the city. They lit the sky ahead of me. By the time I pulled into town the streets were wet, and the only thing that remained to testify to the storm's intensity were a few downed limbs, and scrap paper fluttering, then sticking to the wet street. Once again, the magic of the three rivers had steered the storm around the city.

I stopped at Ralph's.  A light was still on in the family room.  I stopped by my trunk, popped it open, and slid the pistol and ammunition into the trunk.  I slammed the trunk lid. Ralph's back porch light came on. I went around to the sliding door and knocked.  Ralph was dressed in his pajamas.  He let me in.

"What in the world happened to you?"

"Why?"

"Your face is black and you have bean sprouts in your hair."

I told him about the explosion.  Then Ralph exploded. I was engrossed in my own preoccupation.  While he stormed at me about my safety and his sanity,  I wondered where the bean sprouts came from.

## CHAPTER XXI

The next day I returned to Fairview.

I pulled into the filling station. "Can you put a charge on my battery?" I asked.

"Why don't you just let me put a new one in there and tune the thing up?" I'd learned the man's name was Blackie Irelan.

"I've got an appointment to have that done next week."

Blackie just shrugged and went to get the battery charger. He had a long scratch going up the left side of his face that hadn't been there the last time I'd seen him. I left the keys in the ignition and walked to the site of last night's explosion.

I walked toward what was left of the local grain elevator.

The new town marshal was there, as were the state police. I picked my way through the piles of grain and approached a State Trooper standing by his car. I was tempted to tell him I'd witnessed the explosion, but thought better of it, and decided first to find out what the authorities knew.

"What happened here?"

"Well it looks as if it was spontaneous combustion. Sometimes these grains get hot ... gases build up and it just blows sky high."

"Did anyone get hurt?"

"Yeah. We found a body in the office. No identification yet."

"Is it possible it was deliberately blown up?"

"I suppose there's always the possibility, but it's not likely. This sort of thing's happened a lot of places. Elevators just blow up from the grain stored in them."

When he'd mentioned the body, I decided to come clean. I told him I'd received a call from a male voice I didn't recognize asking me to meet him last night at the mill. I described what I saw. He walked me over to a plain-clothes detective who was making notes. He questioned me at length and warned me not to follow up on the sort of invitation I'd gotten last night. He also made me promise to let him

124

know if I found out anything they should know. I had my fingers crossed in my pockets as I promised to listen to him.

"Do you mind if I look around?"

"Sure, just stay away from those other silos. They might not be too stable. Don't go inside any of the buildings."

I wanted to point out the insides of most of the buildings were already outside, but I kept quiet.

I walked back and forth for about half an hour before I found what I was looking for. More bean sprouts. There weren't very many. Just a few here and there. I gathered them up in my hand. There were only about six whole ones, and another half a dozen broken ones. Of course, if they'd been where I think they were, it was surprising this many had survived the explosion. I was just plain lucky one of them had landed in my hair. They tripped a memory of something my sister's boyfriend had been talking about a couple of years ago. They reminded me of the aroma of a barbecue, tomatoes and corn on the cob...and fireworks. But I couldn't figure out what was missing.

I left my name and number with the State Trooper, and asked him to call me if there were any developments. I felt guilty keeping the evidence of the bean sprouts to myself, but also felt sure if I announced I'd found bean sprouts, the least they'd do is look at me funny, and there was the remote possibility they'd question my sanity.

I decided to walk over to the public library. It was a one-story building, with the wonderful smell of books. A tiny woman sat at the desk. I asked to see the high school year books for the past ten years or so. She led me to an alcove where I found fifty years worth of year books all placed on the shelf in chronological order. I started back fifteen years, and worked my way forward. I made a list of people who might be involved. I found pictures of Danny's sisters, and noticed Evelyn was in the same class as Blackie Irelan, the man at the filling station.

I walked back uptown to my car. The keys were lying on the seat and the engine was off, but the battery charger was still attached to the front of the car. I slid under the wheel, picked up the keys and slid them into the ignition. As I gripped the wheel I felt something sticky on my fingers from picking up the keys. The mechanic who put the charger on must have pulled the keys out with grease on his hands or something. I looked at my fingers, but they weren't dirty. I shrugged and waited as the attendant removed the battery charger. I turned the key in the ignition and the car started instantly.

I was sitting in my car, waiting for Fairview's only stoplight to change when someone wrapped their hands around my head, covering my eyes. "Guess who?" I guessed, and I was right.

## CHAPTER XXII

"What are you doing accosting drivers like this?" I asked.

"Couldn't resist. You looked so cute sitting there. What you doing in town today?"

"I heard about the explosion, I wanted to take a look at it."

Gerry jumped into the front seat, and pointed toward the drive-in on the corner, "I'll buy you a Coke."

I pulled in and parked. We ordered drinks and talked until the car hop brought the tray out and set it on the side of the car. This is probably the only place in the world left where you can get curb service. I wondered if he'd seen me in town last night. I was worried he had. But he didn't bring it up, and I didn't ask where he was last night either. We talked for a few minutes, then he asked to take me to a movie that night,

129

and when I agreed, he reached over and tapped the horn, the waitress picked up the tray, and he jumped out of the car the way he'd gotten in.          "See you at 7:00 tonight," he said. He walked over to an old 1989 blue and white Chevy Blazer and pulled the door open.  As he put his foot up to enter, I noticed he was wearing cowboy boots.

I nodded and put the car in gear.  I saw him watching me as I pulled out of the lot, turning down the main drag on the way out of town.

Back in the city again, I headed for the public library on a hunch.  I went to the business and technology section and asked the clerk for some U.S. Army publications.  I couldn't find what I was looking for.

I got into the office about 1:00.  I beat Ralph by ten minutes.  He'd been out of the county at a hearing all morning.  I ran off a couple of pleadings I'd typed the night before and was in the process of stapling them together when he walked past my desk.  He smiled approvingly at all the work I'd gotten done.  If he only knew.  Sometime soon I'd have to bring him up to date on the facts I'd learned, and I'd have to get him to subpoena the records of the Capitol police force on the killing of Rivers' wife and brother-in-law.  I had done a lot of work, and all of it was good.

## CHAPTER XXIII

I had the key in the lock of my front door, when I heard the phone ringing inside.  It was Hazel.  She hung up before I could get to it.

I dialed her number and said "Did you want to talk to me about something?"

"That's really creepy, you know it?"

"It was you that just called me wasn't it?  Besides you do creepy things, too!"

"Yes, but...oh, never mind.  It's about Alice Johnson. I talked to my friend Ethel and she tells me Alice was about to file for divorce.  It seems she and Guy Summerfield were in love years ago.  Guy's first wife died, and he and Alice struck up a friendship again.  The rumor is that's the reason Gerald shot her."

"Do they think Guy's the one who shot Rivers?"

133

"No one thinks he's the type. But then, there's his brother, Norm. He owns the gun shop."

"Could he have done it?"

"Of the two, he'd be the most likely. But why? Guy's a real gentleman. I don't think anyone could imagine him hurting anyone. Norm's more of a mystery."

I filled Hazel in on all of the things I learned in Fairview this morning. She was particularly interested in the happenings in Washington, D. C. She promised to get back to her grapevine information and see if there was anything I'd missed.

"I was in Fairview all morning. I don't suppose you'd want to go back with me tonight?"

"I've got my house to clean, and I have a date tonight."

"A date! That's marvelous."

"You sound like you think it's a miracle I got a date," said the forty-two year old psychic housekeeper.

"No. I think it's wonderful. I've got a date tonight, too."

"You're kidding!" She said. I had it coming.

"Now you sound like you think it's a miracle I got a date."

"Well, you've got to admit you make it hard for guys to

get to know you."

"Name one."

"Who did you turn down last?"

"I guess I've been busy."

"I think you think that's a good excuse."

"I really would like to meet someone. Maybe this guy will work out."

"But it would foul up all of your adventures, wouldn't it?"

"I think I could work them into a relationship."

"Well, I hope this works. Who's the lucky guy?"

"It's Gerry Rivers."

I could hear Hazel's dangly earrings hitting the telephone receiver as she frowned and shook her head. "I don't know. Maybe I'll try to talk you out of this date."

"You don't like him?"

"I never met him. I just don't know..."

"What? Do you know something I don't know?"

"It's just a feeling, the back of my neck tickles thinking about you being with him."

"You're just being an over-protective housekeeper!"

"Be careful, okay?"

I placed the phone back on the receiver. I decided it was too late to run to Fairview and interview Guy Summerfield. As I was getting dressed, I thought about Hazel's neck tickles. As I slipped my little black dress over my head, I had the tickles clear up and down my spine. Just first date jitters, I told myself.

## CHAPTER XXIV

Gerry and I were sitting in my driveway in his little black Chevy pickup truck. He was wearing a black leather jacket. Black leather boots stuck out of the bottom of his black jeans. He looked sexy as hell.

"I like you a lot Poppy. I had a great time."

"I had fun, too, Gerry." It was true, but I felt as if I were crossing my fingers behind my back. There had been fun, but at the same time there was an undercurrent of foreboding running through the whole evening.

He seemed to be a wonderful guy. He showed me more attention in one evening than I'd gotten in the past three years. He was a romantic, bringing me flowers and candy, and taking me to watch the sunset and for a walk on the beach. He was a tender, sensitive man, and would probably have been a wonderful lover. Nevertheless, in the car I kept

137

my purse firmly between us, as a sort of barrier.

For some reason I couldn't figure, I didn't want to commit myself to anything more than a friendship. I wasn't even too sure about that.

"I'm sorry about losing it at the restaurant and parking lot. I've had a lot on my mind lately. I've got to learn to be nicer to people. I think you can help me with that." He'd lost his temper over imagined slights by the waitress at the restaurant, and again with the parking lot attendant. He seemed to be paranoid or to have a persecution complex. The eerie thing about it was he turned into a wild man for a few seconds, then his equilibrium would be restored as if my magic.

"The last few months must have been traumatic for you, losing your stepmother, then your father like that."

"It hurt the most losing Danny as a brother, I guess."

I hadn't seen a specific reason to fear him. I couldn't put my finger on it. When he walked me to my door, I politely turned down his suggestion that he come in. I saw the anger flare again, but just as instantly disappear.

From time to time all evening, he'd skirted around Danny's case, tiptoeing up to ask what we'd learned, and

138

then gliding smoothly away when I said I had a duty of confidentiality. Then ten minutes later he'd skirt around it again. I began to feel as if I should circle the wagons. Although he was terribly polite, something under the surface seemed to be waiting, as if he were going to explode if I didn't "spill the beans." It was decidedly uncomfortable.

At the same time, when I'd try to ease into asking him what he did for a living and why he had so many different cars, he'd change the subject, or act as if he hadn't heard my question. To be fair, I might not have been asking direct questions, either.

When he asked me out again, I was reluctant to commit myself to another date. He was knockout sexy, and various aspects of his appearance made my toes curl, but there was something else...I just couldn't put my finger on it. Maybe Hazel's right. Maybe I'm afraid of commitment, afraid to tie myself down to a normal lifestyle. It might just interfere with my adventures. Finally, I agreed to see him again the next weekend to go to the stock car races.

When I got in the door I took my cell phone out of my purse and put it on the charger. Mousie came over and sniffed my hands, then he walked around and sniffed my purse. He got to the side that had been up against Gerry and went into his bad cat mode. His tail swelled to ten times what it usually was, he turned sideways to the purse and arched his back. He growled at the purse. I grabbed it and put it inside the kitchen cupboard. Mousie calmed down, rubbing himself against my legs as I walked into my living room.

I was on edge later that night, as I went through the house turning off lights, and checking doors and windows. The sound of the fans annoyed me, I couldn't hear anything above their purr. I got up and shut them off, propping my bedroom window open just enough to have a slight breeze. I walked into the kitchen to get a drink of filtered water, and took my cell phone back to the bedroom with me. I put it under my pillow.

I drifted off to sleep, and was awakened by a droning in my ear. I dumped the black furball onto the floor. He gave me a sigh of disgust and left the room. I heard the sounds of the night outside my window. I drifted off to sleep, ready to pull myself back to wakefulness at the next sound, my hand wrapped around my cell phone. I dreamed of the loaded gun still in the trunk of my car.

## CHAPTER XXV

"Excuse me sir. Would you be able to help me jump-start my car?" This was the third stranger I'd accosted this afternoon. He smiled and nodded. Wonderful. Now I could get to Fairview, find Guy Summerfield and find out what he knew.

On the way out of the city I formulated the questions I wanted to ask him. Unfortunately, I didn't get a chance to ask them in the right order. Oh, the bookish, middle-aged man was very pleasant and cooperative, but he wanted to talk about Alice.

"If only I could have gotten her away from him sooner. She was planning to leave him, you know?"

"I've heard rumors." I watched him.

"He was always threatening to kill her." The pain of her death was evident in his appearance. He was months

141

past a good haircut.

"Did you tell the grand jury that?"

"They wouldn't let me testify." He held his hands up helplessly. "I really loved her, you know. She was the most wonderful woman." He twisted his hands.

"They said it was self-defense...when he shot her?"

"Alice wouldn't have done anything to threaten his life. She was talking on the phone to her daughter for God's sakes!"

"When?"

"At the very moment he shot her! Vicky heard the gun shot that killed her mother." Tears were forming in his eyes.

"Do you know what they were talking about."

"She was telling Vicky that she was going to leave Gerald. She told her she still loves me." He threw his hands up in a futile gesture.

"Did you shoot Gerald?"

"No. I wish I'd thought of it...well, I did think of it. I just didn't have the guts to do it." He hung his head.

"Did you talk to Gerald at all after he shot Alice?"

"Yes. I did confront him. He just laughed at me."

"Did you threaten him?"

"Yes. He called me a coward. I suppose I am. If I were braver... Instead Danny had to do the job for me."

"So you think Danny shot him?"

"Danny came to me and told me he was going to do it. I tried to tell him not to ruin his life. ...how proud his mother was of him. ...how much she wanted to get away from Gerald, so he wouldn't be picking on Danny."

"Picking on him? What do you mean?"

"He didn't have anything good to say about anyone. He was always down on somebody. If it wasn't Danny, it was his own son, Gerry."

"Did Danny and Gerry get along all right?

"At first they were together night and day. They seemed to really try to be a family. Gerald couldn't leave them alone. Pitted them against one another all the time. All those contests to see who was the most masculine."

"What kind of contests?"

"Mostly with guns, shooting contests."

"So do you think it was Danny?"

"It looks that way, doesn't it? They say his gun was the one that killed Rivers. I can't say I blame him. Whoever did it, did the world a service."

143

"Did anyone else in town have bad feelings about the town marshal?"

"Nearly everyone. He antagonized everybody."

"How'd he do that?"

"He strutted around town in that western outfit, just like a cowboy marshal out of the old West. He wore that cowboy hat, boots and had two six-shooters strapped on. He liked to push people around. ...intimidate them."

"Besides your feelings, is there anything concrete to make you think Danny killed him?"

"He had every reason to kill him. Yeah, I guess he did it."

"You had every reason to kill him, too."

"Yeah. But I didn't. So Danny must have..."

"I don't think that's the answer I wanted to hear."

"Don't get me wrong. I love Danny like a son. It's just... Well, if there's anything I can do to help Danny, just let me know. Will you tell him I said so?"

"Sure." I watched as Guy Summerfield walked away, his head on his chest. He appeared to have shrunk at least a foot from the time I began the interview. His whole body shook with a deep sigh. He wasn't faking his mourning. It seemed genuine enough.

It was still daylight as I headed out of Fairview. The customary battery charger at the filling station kept me from begging strangers for assistance. Just past the railroad tracks, a light blue pickup truck pulled out of a side road.

A couple of seconds later I was surprised to find myself staring at the nose of it in my rearview mirror. It was right on my bumper. A bearded man, a bright yellow cap pulled down to his eyes, glared at me in the mirror.

Foot on the accelerator, I increased my speed. The pickup stayed right on my bumper. Without taking my right foot from the accelerator, I gently tapped the brake pedal. In the mirror I could see the reflection of my brake lights on the front of the pickup truck. He was too close to see the brake lights!

I slowed down cautiously, hoping he would be bored with following so slow. He shadowed my every move. I felt around in my purse for my cell phone. It was still under my pillow at home.

As we neared the city, I suddenly turned onto a side street without signalling. He slammed on his brakes and followed me. I pulled into a driveway, backed out and went back the way I came, fishtailing around the corner back onto the highway. I passed cars recklessly, swerving to miss oncoming traffic, but I could see him several cars behind me, still following.

As I approached downtown I saw the City Administration Building, and remembered the police garage beneath it. I headed straight for it. I turned the wrong way down a one-way street, and swerved into the entrance to the garage. At the bottom of the ramp I braked to a stop and jumped out. I turned and looked up the ramp. I thought I saw the blue pickup truck drive by slowly.

I jumped from the car to approach the window of the desk sergeant. My legs felt as if they were made of pudding. I grabbed my car door and practised yogic breathing exercises until my heartbeat slowed, and strength returned to my legs.

The desk sergeant sympathized with me, but didn't offer to write up a report. Instead he offered to call Tommy Swift in from the street. Half an hour later, I had a police escort to my front door. At the house, Tommy unlocked the door and went in first. He checked the closets and even knelt down and ran his flashlight under my bed.

146

"Nothing under here but a couple of old boyfriends."

"Sure. I keep a couple of spares around, just in case."

Before he could get to his feet Mousie seductively wiped his body against the dark blue uniform. Now, you'd think that long fluffy black hair wouldn't show on navy blue. Not so. Tommy brushed the monster's fur from his knees, but it didn't do a lot of good. My hairy, little roommate loved men in uniform. Particularly dark uniforms. He seemed to relish jumping into their laps, and shedding truckloads of fur in seconds.

"Looks secure. Lock up and give me a call if you need me...take the invitation any way you want...that's the way I mean it." He put his arm around my shoulders.

"Sure. I'll think about it." I leaned into him. He gave my shoulders a quick squeeze as we both stepped apart.

He picked up the telephone by the door and put it to his ear. "This is okay."

"Thanks Tommy." The phone rang the instant he placed it back on the hook. It was Hazel. He picked it up and handed it to me. Pantomiming locking the door, he waved and left.

## CHAPTER XXVI

"To summarize..." Ralph frowned, then dove beneath the pile of papers on his desk.

"If you'd use the dictating machine you could save time."

"....colon. If the essence of the tort, in law, is non-physical and if the injuries are of the usual non-physical sort...." again, Ralph disappeared under the papers on his desk.

"Ralph are you reading something to me? Ralph? If you are, just give it to me. I can read."

"Here it is....with physical injury being at most added to the list of injuries as a makeweight..."

"You _are_ reading something!" I grabbed the document from his hands. "How much of this do you want me to copy?"

149

"From here to here." He pawed through a dozen pages.

"While I type this, you dictate the rest into the machine. Here it is ready to go." I handed the small recorder to him. He looked at it as if it were a snake about to strike.

I began typing on my keyboard. In the midst of "acts and omissions of the Plaintiff", I suddenly shouted, "Eureka!"

I stored what I'd typed, grabbed my purse and shouted "Bean Bomb! It's a Bean Bomb." I waved to Ralph as I headed for the elevator.

The librarian had the same perplexed look as Ralph when I asked to see Army manuals on bean bombs. I finally remembered it might be in a U.S. Army publication entitled "Booby Traps." She firmly denied that any such publications existed. I gave up and went to Business and Technology. They found the manual almost immediately.

Sure enough, there were instructions for building a timing device for a bomb by placing dry beans into a container and adding water. Eventually the beans would swell and set off the bomb. Apparently the murderer had misjudged the number of beans in his bomb, and they had sprouted before setting off the explosion.

"Do you have any idea who checked this out?"

"I can't say who checked it out. But I can tell you who requested it. I keep a diary."

"Could I see it?"

"Certainly." He handed me a list containing hundreds of names who apparently were requesting hundreds of publications. It looked hopeless.

I handed the roster back and headed for home. Hazel was still there. I explained the bean bomb idea to her, and told her about the roster.

"Why don't you go to the Fairview Library. Maybe they have that publication." She told me the librarian's name was Mrs. Metzger. I waved goodbye and headed for Fairview, after conning Marge into a jump start.

Mrs. Metzger was a tiny woman. She wore half-glasses perched on her nose. She looked up at me over the top of them.

"Why do you require that information, may I ask?"

"I work for Ralph Taylor, Danny Johnson's attorney."

"I see." She hesitated. She looked worried. "It's about bombs, don't you know?"

"Yes. I know. Booby Traps, actually."

"Well, now, I'm not sure it means anything, but there was an explosion. I've wondered about it myself."

"Then you do have the Army manuals?"

"Yes, we have, or had two copies of that publication. In the past year they were checked out three times. Once to Gerald Rivers, Sr., once to Norman Summerfield, and once to Nicholas Roberson, the acting town marshal. I don't recall who didn't return their copy. I suppose it must have been Gerald. He borrowed it before he was shot, 'er killed, 'er murdered. I just hate thinking about poor Alice."

"Did you know Alice well?"

"Her mother and I were schoolmates. I felt like she was my own daughter. I'm very fond of Danny, too. I just can't believe he would murder anyone, anymore than I believe Gerald shot Alice in self-defense. She wouldn't have known how to use a gun."

She wrote the names on the back of a check out card, in a flowing script once known as the Palmer method.

I decided to go see Norm Summerfield. My car started right away...after the nice man at the filling station removed the battery charger.

Norm was busy with a customer. It gave me a chance

to observe him. He was about six foot four, husky, and sported a beard. It was hard to believe that he and Guy were brothers. I thought about the man in the pickup truck. He'd had a beard. It was possible that Norm was older than the man in the pickup truck, however.

"How may I help you?"

"I work for Ralph Taylor, Danny Johnson's attorney."

Norm grabbed a revolver off the counter and held it in front of him. He flipped it open and twirled the cylinder, sighting through the empty chambers. Suddenly he snapped it shut and pointed it at me. "I don't want to talk about the Rivers killing. Just stay out of it."

"I only wanted to ask a couple of questions."

"I don't want to give you any answers. Just get out of town before it's too late."

## CHAPTER XXVII

The next day at noon, I met with the State Police recruiter who had processed Danny's application to join the ranks of the State Troopers. He was very impressed with Danny's scores, and with his psychological tests. He'd been surprised when he learned that Danny was the prime suspect in the murder of his step-father.

"Frankly, if he's guilty, I'll be really surprised."

"Did the State Police investigate the murder of Danny's mother, Alice Rivers?"

"Yes. We always get called in to investigate when there's a law enforcement officer involved with a killing. Particularly in a case like this where he was the only law enforcement officer."

"Can you tell me why the grand jury didn't bring, at

155

least, manslaughter charges against Gerald Rivers for Alice's death?"

"Basically, because it was his word against nothing. There was a gun laying on the floor next to her body. He claimed she'd pointed it at him, and he'd shot her in self-defense."

"How far away was he when he shot her?"

"The other side of the room. Her gun's safety was on when we found it."

"Didn't that make you wonder?"

"Well, she'd had no experience with guns, but it did make me wonder; but I wasn't conducting the investigation, and apparently it seemed reasonable to the grand jury. They didn't indict him."

"And then he was killed, so that was the end of that."

"Pretty much the way it happened. I suspect from what I'd heard that if he'd lived longer, evidence might have come out that would have brought it back up again."

"You mean he could have been indicted for her murder, if he'd not been murdered?"

"It was a good possibility. Someone rushed the grand jury hearing before all the evidence had been gathered."

"What about the evidence against Danny. Is there more than circumstantial evidence?"

"Yeah. There's his rifle and the slug that matches that they took out of Gerald River's body. Plus, he had motive and he had opportunity."

"That doesn't necessarily mean he did it though, does it?"

"They can make a pretty good case. It'll be up to a jury to decide if there's a reasonable doubt."

"Do you know if the State Police have investigated anyone else in Gerald Rivers' murder?"

"Almost everyone had an idea of who might have done it. Since I'm not working on the investigation, I don't know how many leads they followed up. I know they spent quite a lot of time on it at first, until they found the bullet matched Danny Johnson's rifle."

"You mean, they stopped looking after that?"

"I don't know, but they probably did."

I thanked him for his time, and headed back to work. You'd have thought I'd been gone for years. Ralph was having a snit. I pretended I was properly chastened and worked hard the rest of the day.

157

## CHAPTER XXVIII

The phone rang at work the next day. It was that handsome State Trooper I'd met at the grain elevator explosion.

"Hello! It's good to hear from you."

"Hello? Is this Ms. Hannah? This is Lt. Duffy of the State Police."

"I know. What can I do for you?"

"Well, we've identified the body found in the grain elevator. It was an old man everyone calls Shorty."

"I had a feeling. What do you think he was doing there?"

"Well, the theory is he was just trying to get out of the rain, but he only lived two blocks away. Then again, some say his house was flooded, being so close to the river."

"I'd just talked to him the day before the explosion.

159

You don't think someone was trying to shut him up?"

"If they were, then you'd be better off to just stay out of things. Don't do anything dumb. It's a police matter now. If he told you anything important, it'd be best if you just tell us what you know and let us handle it. You don't want to be guilty of obstructing justice, do you?"

Just as I replaced the phone on the receiver from that call, Kara told me I had a call on line two. I took it.

"This is Mr. Taylor's paralegal, can I help you?"

A hesitant female voice asked, "Are you Poppy Hannah?"

I assured her I was. She made a couple of false starts, and then blurted out. "I think I might know who killed the town marshal."

I asked her if I could come and talk to her. She gave me her address. I was surprised. It wasn't the sort of address you would expect from an informant. It made me wonder what she wanted to tell me, and what her motive was in telling me. She said her name was Margaret Lafferty. I recognized the name. Her husband was one of the men in the boss's foursome at the last charity golf tournament. Ralph had been duly impressed to be playing golf with such a high roller.

I'd just hung up the phone when it rang again. This time I didn't know who it was. Someone I haven't met yet, obviously.

## CHAPTER XXIX

"Meet me at the Talking Parrot." said a male voice. I didn't recognize it. But when I heard it I thought of Guy Summerfield. It wasn't him, but it made me think of him.

At any rate, it was someone who knew where to find me. I jumped up to tell Ralph.

"You're going to stay here and type that brief for me."

"But Ralph, it's a lead. Someone wants to talk to me."

"It could be anything. You've got a job here, and I told you before to stay out of this. It's getting too dangerous."

"Yes, Ralph." Better to let him think I was giving up, rather than get another lecture about staying out of things.

I thought of a couple dozen excuses for leaving work early, but I'd already used most of them, so it was nearly 4:30 before I could get away from the office. Kara promised to cover for me. I had to go home and get some things, and

163

then I had to feed the Big Black Furry. While I was there Hazel called, and then my mother called, and I talked to her for awhile because she complained I hadn't really talked to her in a long time. We watched Wheel of Fortune together, and solved a puzzle or two. Then I told her I had to go. Before going to Fairview, I had an appointment to talk to someone about Danny's case.

# CHAPTER XXX

I found my way to the better part of town, and pulled into the long driveway of a custom-designed split-level, professionally landscaped house. I left the car running, so I wouldn't be embarrassed by that recalcitrant battery when I left. I rang the bell. The door was opened by a slightly built blond. She was dressed in a very simple silk pantsuit, with a gold chain circling her tiny waist. Gold chains were hidden in the folds of the neckline. Long gold herringbone earrings hung from her ears and showed off her long neck. She was tiny but perfectly proportioned. A very large diamond dwarfed her small hand. She should have had long glamorous nails, but it appeared that she had chewed hers down to the quick.

"You must be Poppy," she said as she took my arm and pulled me into the house. Her name was Marianne Rupley. Hazel's friend had suggested that Marianne might know something. When I'd called to make the appointment,

165

she'd seemed alternately eager and reluctant to talk to me. She quickly shut the door and motioned for me to follow her. The scent of Georgio, wafted behind her as she walked. We stepped across a white-tiled floor into a library I would love to have. I glanced quickly around the room at the titles. It was heavenly. There were floor to ceiling books lining all of the walls, except the outside wall, which was glass. The roof overhang was very deep, casting shadows into the room, and beyond the flagstone patio outside there was a lush garden area. It was so heavenly. I said that before. Well, it was my dream house.

"Where's your husband?" I asked.

She waved her hand as if to dismiss my question, pulled out a small white barrel chair and motioned for me to sit. She took a twin chair across a small glass table. Suddenly she jumped up. "Can I get you something to drink?"

"No, I'm fine. I can't stay long." I motioned for her to sit. She did.

She jumped up again and closed the library door, and came back and sat down. She looked around nervously. "Well, I don't know if this is worth anything or not. You see, I used to see Gerry Rivers when his Dad was still alive. I knew

166

Danny Johnson, too. Gerry and I went together. I don't want anyone to know that, though. I was married then. I still am. I mean, well..."

She jumped up again, and paced back and forth from the glass doors to the library door, wearing a path in the carpet as she told me about Gerry's cocaine habit.

"I don't know whether he's still using or not." She went on to explain. "he becomes a completely different person when he's under the influence of cocaine. It worries me the criminals he'd contact for a hit when he was into using. Do you think he's still using?" she asked.

"I'm not sure I'd be able to tell. I don't know him that well."

"He takes a lot of chances. His judgment isn't the best. I think his Dad found out. I wonder if the guys he was hanging out with to get the coke had anything to do with Gerald being killed." She said she felt responsible for this, since she had been the one who had insisted that Gerry clean up his act.

"I'm sure that Gerry wouldn't have killed his dad. They didn't get along so well, but I think Gerry loved him," she said.

I thanked her for the information, and sneaked a peak

at the rest of the house, as she led me back to the front door. She told me to call her during the day, if there was anything else I needed to know. She cautioned me not to call on the weekend. She mentioned her husband was out of town for a couple of days, but he was getting back the next afternoon.

"John knows I was involved with Gerry. You see, I was a user, too. I'm clean now. I don't want to make it any harder on John. You understand?" she asked.

She looked troubled as she closed the door.

I still had to make it to Fairview.

## CHAPTER XXXI

By the time I pulled into Fairview the sun was getting close to the horizon. I went into the Talking Parrot and sat down in a booth. There were only a couple of other people in there sitting at the bar. One of them, looking a lot like a fugitive from a motorcycle gang, gave me the eye, and the other was an old farmer who was nursing a draft beer.

The biker boy picked up his drink and wandered over to my table. The bartender came right behind him and waved the bar rag at the table.

"Bring me a club soda with a twist of lemon, please."

"Wow, that's a bit hefty for a little girl like you. How 'bout lettin' me buy you a real drink." said the biker.

"No thank you."

"You're new around here aren't you?"

"Did you have something important you wanted to say

169

to me."

His reply was rude, but made it clear that <u>this</u> was not the mystery caller. I said, "I'm waiting for my lover, she's late."

Warding off the plague, he held up both hands and backed toward the bar. The bartender brought my club soda, forgetting the lemon twist.

I sat in the booth long enough to see the sun set. No one showed up, so I walked back toward the filling station where my battery was getting it's daily boost.

As Blackie removed the battery charger he made his now familiar sales pitch, "Can't I put a new battery in there for you, and give you a tune up?"

"No, I've got an appointment next week to have that done."

I headed out of town with my headlights on, the sky growing darker behind me.

I had the radio tuned to some jazz, and I'd spaced out grooving to the music, when suddenly I was jolted back to reality by something hitting the rear of my car. In the rearview mirror I could make out the hood ornament of a Cadillac. I hit the brakes and saw their red reflection on the front of the white car. It was my old friend the White Cadillac again. I sped up to get away from him, and swerved into a curve, throwing gravel off the side of the road. He remained right on my tail, still driving without any lights.

I decided to try my old ploy and tapped the brakes. It didn't faze him. I hit them again, and he rammed me hard. I lost control and saw myself heading for the ditch.

## CHAPTER XXXII

I hurt all over! My head was killing me. As I reached to feel my head, I touched a bandage on my forehead. I feared I was blind, I couldn't see a thing. I wasn't blind. I was in the dark, somewhere. I was lying on a cot of some kind, and it smelled damp and musty, wherever I was.

"Oh, that hurts." I sat up and tried to swing my feet over to the side. They hit a wall. I turned and swiveled the other direction. I could see a faint light coming from high on the wall.

I groped around with my hands and found a small table next to the cot or couch I'd been lying on. There was a small lamp there. I fumbled for the light switch. There it was. The lamp cast a welcoming circle of light upon me and my environment. It was a gloomy looking place, no ambiance at all.  I figured the light must have been moonlight coming through a high set window.  It appeared I was in somebody's basement.

It took me a while to figure out why I was there and how I got there.  Then I remembered the white Caddy, and being forced into a ditch.  Apparently someone had kidnaped me and was holding me for ransom in this basement!

I stood up and held the small lamp above my head to throw light on the entire basement.  I looked for my purse, and my cell phone.  They didn't appear to be with me.  I felt in the pocket of my jacket.  Empty.

There was a set of stairs leading up on the other side of the room.  I removed the lampshade from the lamp, set it back on the table and slowly made my way toward the stairs.  Suddenly I heard the crunch of tires on gravel.  I ran back to the lamp and switched it off.  I knocked something off the table as I set the lamp back down.  I found I was holding my breath as I listened carefully.  A car door slammed.  I lay back down on the cot, and pulled the sheet up over myself, slowly turning with my back to the stairs, trying to control my breathing.  I heard the door at the top of the stairs open before I saw the wall behind me light from above.  I realized I was holding my breath and tried to breathe naturally as if I were asleep. I observed the light moving as if a flashlight were being played around the room. The light switched off and I heard the door close.

Shivers ran down my spine as I let out my breath. I heard footsteps overhead, and then a door closing, and boards creaking as someone walked across the porch. The screen door screeched as it opened, and then its spring pulled it shut with a snap. In the distance I heard a car engine start and the crunch of gravel as it left.

I listened carefully and didn't hear any other sounds. Believing myself to be alone once again, I switched the light back on. I looked at my hands. They were shaking.

I went to the window dragging a small stool with me. I set it beneath the window and climbed up. The window was dirty. I rubbed a spot clean so I could look out. The yard outside was illuminated by a light from somewhere to my right. There in the yard sat my car. The right front fender was bashed in where it hit the ditch. I groaned. I'd just finished paying for the last damage, and I couldn't remember if I'd made my insurance premium payment that month.

Suddenly, again, I heard the crunching sound of a

175

vehicle on gravel, and the yard was swept with bright lights. I quickly ran to the lamp and turned it off. The sound of clanking chains stirred my curiosity and I crept back to the window. It was a wrecker. On the side of it in big red letters it said, "Tony's Wrecker Service". It hooked up to my car and towed it away. The night grew very still again.

My heart was beating rapidly. My mouth was dry. And I had the hiccups. I found my way back to the lamp and clicked it on. I went to the refrigerator in the corner and opened the door. There was a lot of lunchmeat. Whoever had left me there didn't know I was a vegetarian. There was a pitcher of orange juice. I drank directly from the pitcher. I still had the hiccups. I put the pitcher back and noticed a canister of water. I poured a glassful into a paper cup and took it back to the cot and set the cup on the table.

Maybe the guy left the door unlocked, I thought. I ran towards the stairs, and galloped up two at a time. It was locked. I grabbed the doorknob and rattled it. "Hey, let me out."

Frightened the wrong person might have heard me I scurried down the stairs and back over to the cot, switched out the light and lay down. My mouth was fuzzy now. I listened for about thirty seconds, then reached for the cup. Just as I reached for it I hiccuped and the water sloshed over the rim. I tipped it up and drained it. It nearly came back up as I hiccupped again.

Whatever happened to the theory that fear would rid one of the hiccups? Miserably I sat on the edge of the cot, the steel edge cutting into the back of my legs as I tried to think what to do. Each thought was rudely interrupted by the next hiccup. I switched the light back on, stood up and found myself a bit dizzy. Probably from trying to stare into the darkness or something. Or maybe lack of air from these stupid hiccups, I thought. I poured myself another glass of water, swallowed it quickly, holding my breath. Another hiccup. I took the water canister back to the cot with me, tipped it up and chugged it all down. The hiccups were gone. I should put the canister away, I thought. I stood up to go back to the refrigerator and the world turned upside down. Trying to catch myself, I dragged the still lighted lamp from the table. We all fell to the floor, the table, the lamp and me, like humpty dumpty.

## CHAPTER XXXIII

I heard tires scrunching on the gravel outside. I opened my eyes to see bright sunshine sweeping through the small basement window. My head hurt. I was on the cot, all tucked in. Pain shot through my temples as I turned my head toward the table next to the cot. The table was upright, and the lamp was sitting thereon. Unlit. Someone has put us all together again.

Slowly I pushed the blanket from me and swung my legs over the side of the cot. There must have been a drug in the water.

I heard footsteps on the porch, and heard the door opening. I swung myself back into the cot, with my back to the stairs. I held my breath. The footsteps proceeded overhead and to the cellar door. The door creaked open. I could hear breathing, and then the door closed again. I listened for the click of the lock, but it didn't come.

The footsteps went back the way they came, and then I heard a car door slam, and an engine start. Gravel crunched as the vehicle left.

Holding my throbbing head, I jumped up and ran to the small window to look out. There on the driveway sat my car. The fender was no longer bashed in!

I raced up the stairs and tentatively turned the doorknob. It opened without any problem. I listened in the house. It smelled as musty upstairs as it did in the basement. I found my way to the front door and tried the doorknob. This door was unlocked as well. There in front of the house sat my car, looking bright and shiny and new. Walking around it I could find no evidence it had been damaged. Maybe I was dreaming when I thought someone had towed it away? But then I could smell fresh paint. I ran my hand over the fender. It felt slightly tacky. I tried the door, and it was unlocked. The keys were in the ignition. My purse sat on the seat where I always kept it. My cell phone rested in the outside pocket of the purse. The purse looked neater than it did before. Sure enough, it had been organized. Everything was very neatly packed into it. I opened the billfold. I knew I'd had a dollar bill and about fifty cents in change. There were five twenties, and a one dollar bill. In the coin purse there was fifty cents. What? I've been paid to be kidnaped?

I turned and looked on the floor of the back seat. It was no longer a rolling garbage can. Someone had cleaned it out. I could smell the artificial aroma of lilac from the car wash.

Well, they didn't fix the battery, so I'll be stuck here anyway, I thought. I was about to turn the key in the ignition when it occurred to me that someone might have gone to these elaborate lengths to get rid of me. Maybe they cut the brake lines or maybe they put a bomb in it. I climbed back out and threw the hood up. I traced all of the wires to their source, or as close as I could come. Except for the cables to the battery, they all looked pretty old. I was back into the car before the new battery cables made an impression. I pulled the hood release and ran to the front of the car, again. I struggled to lift the hood. I can't say I was surprised to see the new battery.

Not knowing precisely what I was looking for, I crawled under the front of the car and looked at where I thought the brakes might be. Everything looked dirty and old there, too.

181

Nothing looked like it had been tampered with or freshly cut.

Back in the driver's seat, I held my breath as I turned the key and the engine jumped to life. I let out the clutch and the car crept forward, I pretended the accelerator was made of glass. The car swept down the drive. Not even a rattle.

Now what? I'd thought I'd be able to go to the F.B.I. with great drama and describe my kidnaping. Now what was I going to tell them? "Someone forced me off the road and kidnaped me so they could put a new battery in my car and clean my purse?"

## CHAPTER XXXIV

It was a beautiful day. I'd always imagined kidnaping would be more traumatic. Can't say that I minded it a bit, now the feeling of sheer terror was over. Before I made my way back to town, I turned on Navigation on my cell phone, and opened My Tracks to make a map as I went home to show where I'd been held captive.

I had the slight feeling of being followed, but I didn't see anything out of the ordinary. In fact, there were few cars on the road at all.

As I rolled into the driveway, I noticed everything looked normal. It was sort of disconcerting to find there were no police tape lines around the house. Nobody seemed to have noticed I'd been missing.

Just then Marge came running out of her house. "Where have you been all weekend?!"

"You'll never believe this, but someone kidnaped me."

Marge listened while I told her the details. She was okay until I told her the part about them stealing my car and bringing it back fixed.

"What?" I asked when I saw the incredulous expression on her face.

"You don't remember?"

"What?"

"Last week. You said, 'I wish someone would steal this darn thing and fix it for me.'"

"Oh....I did didn't I."

"You'd better watch what you wish from now on. I'm glad you made it back okay."

I handed Marge's jumper cables back to her, and walked to my door. I turned the key in my lock, and the big black furball leapt off the counter at me. I ducked and he rolled across the floor. With great dignity, he turned and with one huge "meow", told me he'd planned his little maneuver to work out that way. There was a note from Hazel on the kitchen table. I dialed her number as I opened a can of tuna for the Mouse.

Hazel was the only other person I wasn't afraid to tell

about the latest adventure. She wouldn't approve, but she'd believe me. I'm not sure anyone else would. At any rate, she was the only one I could tell. Ralph would lock me up.

When she offered to come over and keep me company for awhile, I accepted. I felt more than a little rattled by all of this. Though it appeared I'd been treated well, and come out of the deal better than when I went in, I needed a little babying from Hazel. It couldn't hurt.

Hazel arrived within minutes. She moved around my little house fluffing up pillows and dusting, while I took a shower.

"I was worried when you didn't come home, so I came over to feed the cat." She handed me a fluffy towel as I stepped out of the shower.

"Did Ralph call?" I asked, as I began picking at my mop of curls, trying to loosen them up. They looked like a Brillo pad.

"No, but Elizabeth did. You'd promised to come over and play paper dolls with her this weekend."

"What did you tell her?" I pulled on a house coat and followed Hazel to the kitchen.

"That you had a date." Hazel started dragging food

from the refrigerator, and I popped a muffin into the microwave for a few seconds.

"Oh, boy. That should be interesting. Ruth is always trying to get me married off." I found some cream cheese for my muffin.

"So, how was your date the other night?"

"It was okay, I just didn't feel real comfortable with him. He came right out and asked me though if I knew who'd killed his Dad."

"What did you tell him."

"I told him I wasn't psychic, and hadn't figured it out yet."

Hazel raised an eyebrow at that. "Have you asked your angels about this one yet?"

"Yeah, whenever I ask, 'Who killed Gerald Rivers', they just echo, 'Gerald Rivers'".

"What, he committed suicide?"

"No, he didn't. That's why I just dismiss the answer. It doesn't make any sense."

"So. What are we going to do about your little adventure?" Asked Hazel, as she handed me a cup of tea.

"What's to do? No one will believe me." I watched as

Hazel pulled more food from the refrigerator and began cleaning vegetables. I told her about keeping a record of the way home on My Tracks. I was afraid if I showed her, I'd lose the evidence somehow.

"The first thing it seems would be to locate that Tony's Wrecker Service." She sliced vegetables like a chef selling woks on television.

"I already Googled it. There's no listing. It's a dead end." I pressed my thumb down on the crumbs remaining on my plate and licked them off my finger. I was still famished.

"It's not what you know, but who you know who knows what you need to know that'll get the job done." said Hazel, emphasizing each word with a whack of her cleaver on some poor, defenseless, carrots.

By the time Hazel cleared up the kitchen and went home, I'd eaten a gorgeous salad, and a melt-in-your-mouth vegetable quiche. And that was just lunch. A marvelous macaroni casserole was cooking slowly in the oven, and there was a loaf of oatmeal bread rising on the counter. A plate of sliced tomatoes covered with saran wrap, and a covered green bean casserole waited in the refrigerator. I was in heaven.

## CHAPTER XXXV

I was awakened early Monday morning by a telephone call from Hazel. She'd learned Tom Wright had purchased Tony's wrecker and started his own wrecker service. He'd never changed the name on the side of the wrecker, but it was now listed in Fairview's phone directory as Tom's Wrecker Service. I planned another trip to Fairview to investigate.

But first I had to get into the office and get some work done. Ralph was in Court all day. He called me from the Courthouse and asked me what I'd been doing all day. I told him about a couple of things.

"Is that all?" he asked. It wasn't all, but I couldn't remember what else I'd done. It had been quite a lot actually. I don't know what he thinks I'm doing, but he's always asking for lists. Even if I could make a list, I'd probably forget seventy-five percent of what I've done. If I kept a list, I'd be

189

spending all my time keeping lists instead of getting the work done. I just do it and get it out of my sight.

Then I made the mistake.

"Oh, by the way," I told him, "I had a bit of an adventure last Friday night." I told him the rest of the story. I could hear him sputtering. He told me to wait right there at the office until he got out of Court. He was so upset with me his voice squeaked.

When Ralph got back to the office he insisted I go home with him. Ruth fixed a wonderful dinner, and hustled the kids off to bed early. They were complaining, but I promised I'd tuck them in and tell them a story. Anything to put off the lecture.

It didn't turn out as bad as I thought. Ralph tried to lecture, but Ruth wouldn't let him. She wanted me to tell her the whole story. Although Ralph didn't see it that way, she tended to agree with me, whoever kidnaped me felt guilty about it, and changed his mind, and I was probably not in any danger from that quarter.

Ralph never really agreed with us, and finally just before he dropped me at home, he got his lecture in. He told me to forget about Danny and the investigation and let the professionals do the investigating.

In the darkened car, with fingers crossed, I promised I'd stay out of it.

As I opened my back door, the phone rang. It was Ruth.

"Hello Ruth." I said. "Did I forget something?"

"Oh Poppy. I just wanted to make sure to tell you to lock the doors good, and listen to Ralph. We'd all be very sad to lose you."

I promised to be very careful, and hung up the phone. There was a note from Hazel on the refrigerator. It was the phone number for Tom's Wrecker Service.

I called and learned Tom only worked nights and weekends because he had a full-time day job in a factory. He told me he didn't have anyone around to watch his kids tonight, and couldn't make a run to pick up my "wrecked" car, but if I could wait until tomorrow night he'd drag it to my garage for me, and the price would be worth waiting.

I asked him for his address, and told him I'd call him back after I'd checked around to see if I could get it done sooner.

I had a spooky feeling as I pulled open the door to my

closet to get my housecoat. I couldn't put my finger on the feeling, but it prompted me to check all of my doors and windows. I threw all of the deadbolts, and put the chains on the doors. I even went down the basement and checked the windows. A year ago when there'd been a lot of burglaries in the neighborhood, I'd installed brackets on each side of the windows I could drop a two by four into, forming a sort of barrier  so no one could slip through the window without making a lot of noise, and without a lot of trouble. They were all in place, but I got a hammer and some ten penny nails and toenailed them into the window frames on both sides.   I noticed the floor was wet around the sump pump, and the hole I'd dug for the pump was muddy. I got mud on my shoes from standing there pounding the nails into the window frame.

 I ought to get around to cleaning up the pile of mud one of these days.

As I was going back up the stairs I saw a muddy footprint that hadn't come from my shoes on the bottom step. It looked like the print a rather large cowboy boot would have made.   I looked at the print for a full minute, wondering how it could have gotten there.   It was dried mud, but it was definitely mud.  I knew Hazel always swept the basement stairs as one of her weekly chores. She griped at me constantly to clean up the mud in the basement. I'd been thinking of hiring someone to carry the dirt out for me.

I called Hazel and asked her if she'd had anyone in the house over the weekend wearing cowboy boots. She hadn't. I called Tommy. He was there in twenty minutes. What I really wanted was for someone to sweep the house for fingerprints, and tell me right then and there who'd been in my house, but all I got was a very thorough security check to make sure I was in, and everybody else was out. That didn't help a lot, since there was no sign of breaking and entering. Whoever had been in my house had gotten in with a key. It was either the guys who kidnaped me, or it could have happened when I left the keys in my car at the garage in Fairview with the battery charger hooked up. Someone had made a duplicate. The keys to the office were also on that key ring. I debated whether or not to tell Ralph about that, and decided not to bother. After all, they'd come here, not the office. So far as I could figure they hadn't tossed the office. And they'd done a very careful search of my house. I didn't notice anything out of place until after I'd found there'd been someone there. Nothing was missing, so far as I could see.

193

Tommy stayed around and checked all of the locks, and put another chain lock on the back door for me. I was standing, leaning against the counter in the corner next to the door, watching him work. He turned suddenly, put his arms on both sides of me and kissed me. I kissed him back. It very effectively erased all of the doubts and fears residing in my brain up until that very second. Unfortunately, they all came rushing back the second he stopped.

"You made me stop worrying for awhile," I told him.

"I can keep you from worrying all night long, if you like."

I ducked under his left arm and stood in the middle of the kitchen. "It sounds like a wonderful idea, but..."

"Yeah, I know. I guess that's why I keep trying. You keep saying no."

"If I said yes, you might stop coming around."

"I might not, too."

He kissed me again, and I tried not to encourage him. He turned and left. I smiled and locked the door. Darn. He is sweet, I thought.

I went to bed thinking of Tommy, and drifted right off to sleep. I was dreaming of palm trees and a soft breeze blowing my hair when I was awakened by a dreadful shriek, and at the same time my bed bounced as if an earthquake had struck. As I sat up to switch on the light, something crashed against the side of my bed again. And then a soft voice said "Herrroooo." It was Mousie my talking cat. He was waking me up. He'd done it before when the lawn furniture was stolen off my patio awhile back.

I got up, grabbed my cell phone, and switched on the flashlight app. I held the lit side to my chest until I had walked as far as I could in the dark. I went from window to window listening. Finally I bravely turned the light outward to check in the shadows of the living room. Mousie's eyes glowed in the light of the cell phone. He looked like an alien. But there were no shadows anywhere in my house, and there were no noises outside. I thought of opening the back door and looking to see if everything was on the patio, but I didn't. I peeked through the curtain over the sliding door, and saw nothing but the soft glow of the white furniture. I glanced down and saw the broomstick I always put in the door so it couldn't be slid open was in place.

I jumped as Mousie brushed up against the back of my legs. I picked him up and carried him back to bed. We slept peacefully the rest of the night.

## CHAPTER XXXVI

The first thing next morning the phone rang. It was Ralph.

"Hi Ralph, what's up."

"You are. You and Ruth and the kids are booked on a flight to Washington, D.C. I can't go. You're going to go and help Ruth with the kids, and take a vacation."

"I've already had a vacation, Ralph."

"You've got another one."

"Is this with pay?"

"Of course."

"Okay, but I have some work to do in Fairview today."

"The plane leaves in three hours."

"I'd better pack."

"You're learning."

197

"Thanks Boss."

I hung up and called Hazel.

"Hello Poppy."

"Wow, you can do it, too."

"Did you know you're going on a long trip?"

"I just found out."

"Stay out of trouble.  I see some trouble for you. There's going to be some danger."

"You're full of good news."

"Just be careful.  When do you get back?"

"Apparently this is just going to be for four days.  Can you feed the Mouse?"

"You know I can."

"Be sure to lock everything up real good and keep an eye on things."

"You got it sweetie.  Stay out of trouble."

## CHAPTER XXXVII

We landed at the Washington Airport at Noon. We were supposed to take a taxi to a Holiday Inn in Alexandria. According to Ralph it was located right next to a metro station, which we could take to the city to explore. Ruth and I talked it over and decided it would be more practical to have a vehicle. So we rented a mid-size car and drove straight to the hotel. It was easy. We checked into our rooms, changed clothes, packed the kids in the car and took off with me at the wheel.

"Are all the bridges alike?" asked Elizabeth?

We got lost quite a lot. I didn't know there were so many bridges between Washington and Virginia. We finally crossed the Mason Memorial Bridge, and took an off ramp that looked as if it might lead to the Lincoln Memorial.

"There it is, the Lincoln Memorial. That's where we'll go first." I said. Somehow we found ourselves at the Jefferson Memorial instead.

"That doesn't look like Abraham Lincoln." said Elizabeth.

"It's Thomas Jefferson," offered Julia. "We studied him in school."

We got out, took pictures, explored, and got back in the car, and attempted to head for the Washington Monument.

"This road will take us to the Washington Monument," I announced.

We reached the Lincoln Memorial, got out and wandered around. Elizabeth looked up and said, "That's Abraham Lincoln!"

"Aberbam Limcome." said Teddy. Julia frowned and took his hand.

We climbed up and had our pictures taken with Abe, and asked where the Smithsonion was located. Following a pointed finger, we happened upon the Vietnam Veteran's Memorial, and a cool park-like atmosphere.

"This isn't the Smithsonian," said Elizabeth. "We studied about this in school. This is the Vietnam Memorial.

200

Those are the names of everyone who died."

Teddy was bored, and Julia was sad.

We decided the Washington Monument and the Smithsonian were too far away for walking, found our way back to the car, and while I thanked the angels for our next parking spot near the Washington Monument, Ruth looked at the map. I quickly tapped on my Navigation app and got directions. With the help of the lady on the navigation I drove straight to the Washington Monument, pulled into a parking spot just as it was being vacated, and we walked to the bottom of the monument.

"Wow, you really found it Poppy." said Elizabeth. She seemed disappointed.

"Didn't you want to find it?" I asked.

"It's kind of fun the other way. I like surprises." said Elizabeth.

We took pictures, went inside, discouraged Teddy from a climb, and came back out. The Smithsonian looked much closer, but again, parking nearby was to our advantage. We climbed back into our car, relinquished our parking spot to another lucky tourist, and drove down 17th Street past the statue of John Paul Jones, turned onto Jefferson Drive, took a side street, and parked directly behind the Smithsonian. We walked through several beautiful gardens, into the castle where we picked up information about the museums. We decided the children would most enjoy the Natural History Museum across the mall. When we reached the center, we stopped and posed for pictures, two with the Capitol in the background, and two with the Washington Monument in the background. We stepped over a number of people who appeared to be sleeping in the center of the mall.

After a fast tour through many halls, we stopped in a Cafeteria in the basement of the Natural History Museum and had drinks and a snack. While Ruth cleaned up the kids, I made a telephone call to one of Gerald Rivers' old neighbors, and made an appointment to meet her that evening in Georgetown. I then telephoned the law firm on the letterhead I'd found in Gerald's bottom drawer and asked to speak to the attorney who'd written to Gerald. We made an appointment to speak the next day.

We made it back to our rooms, laden down with packages of souvenirs. Ruth wanted to get the kids cleaned up, and I wanted to make another phone call. We met in the lobby, and went out to a local restaurant for a light supper. I dropped Ruth and the kids off at the hotel.

"I'll see you guys in the morning." I said.

"Where are you going, Poppy?" asked Ruth.

"I'm just going to go by and see a friend I went to school with.  She lives in Georgetown." I said.  I really do have a friend who lives in Georgetown.  I really did mean to call her if I had the time.  First I had to go talk to Gerald's neighbor.  I had my fingers crossed.

"Well, I don't suppose it will do any harm.  Just be very careful.  Remember this is not home."  Ruth said.

# CHAPTER XXXVIII

I'd expected Rita Printz to be much older. She was only about thirty-five years old and very attractive. We found a table in the rear of a restaurant on a crowded side street. We both ordered tea.

"How long did you know the Rivers Family?" I asked.

"I moved next door about six months before Mrs. Rivers was killed. I didn't know her very well."

"Did you know Gerald?" I asked.

"No, I didn't know him well either." She seemed reluctant to go on.

"Then I guess I just need to ask, what do you know that could help me figure out who killed Gerald?"

"I don't know that either. Well." She stopped and looked around.

I waited.

"I know about the drug things that were going on." She

stopped again.

Waiting seemed to work.

"I hate to tell you this. Do you know Gerry?"

"Yes."

"Do you know how old he is?"

"I guess he's about twenty-five." I said.

"He's twenty-six. That's how old I was, when I met him."

I still didn't understand what she was trying to say.

"He told me he was twenty-one. He was only seventeen."

I waited.

"He was the best lover I've ever had."

I waited longer, while I tried to get my lower jaw to stop hanging down.

"I really didn't know how old he was. He was so experienced, and he was so good. I introduced him to some people, and through them he met some other people. He got really involved with alcohol and drugs. I have to admit I was into drugs then too. I've been clean for five years."

I nodded, afraid if I said much she'd stop talking.

"We were trying to make a score one night...in a really

206

bad neighborhood. We were sitting in the car. It was dark. We were waiting outside this house, and we saw one of the big guys pull up. He got out, and turned to talk to someone in the car, and another car pulled up right beside them. A guy got out with an automatic pistol and killed him. The last thing I remember before they pulled away was looking directly into his face. I swear he saw us, but he just left."

"How did you know he was 'one of the big guys'?"

"I don't know. That's what Gerry told me, I guess."

"How did he know?"

"I'm not sure. Anyway, we were in Gerry's Uncle's car. We took off and left.        Then a couple weeks later, Gerry's mother was murdered, and a week after that his Uncle was murdered. I took a leave of absence from my job and went back to Wisconsin for three months. When I came back Gerry and his Dad had moved away. I didn't really know where they'd gone until some insurance guy came around asking questions."

"Did he try to sell you insurance?" I asked, trying to lighten the mood.

"Yeah, he did." She laughed.

"Do you know if anyone has ever been charged in the

murder you witnessed?"

"No, I've been afraid to find out. I feel so guilty I never went to the police."

We paid for our drinks, and walked out. She walked me toward my rental car. As we approached we saw a street person reach out to the white car and pull on the handle. As I was about to shout to the man to stay away from my car, it exploded. The white driver's door flew straight out from the car, catching the man in the torso. He and the door were flung across the street. The screeching of metal on metal and his screams intermingled. The force of the explosion upon the man and door, caused them to both slide under a car on the other side of the street.

Then a miracle occurred. The man crawled out from under the car, stood up, brushed himself off and hobbled away. His hat was lying on the street in flames. My rental car, what was left of it, was also in flames. It didn't take long for the fire department and the police to arrive. My companion begged to be allowed to leave. She didn't want to be seen with me. I let her go, after I found more than one other person had witnessed the explosion.

I was questioned by the police. A very nice uniformed

police officer, Don Tharpe, introduced himself to me, and took my arm. He walked me back inside the restaurant, and found a secluded table where we sat and talked.

"I shouldn't have come over here, I guess." I said.

"Do you have any idea who did this?"

"No, but I might have an inkling why." I said.

I explained why I'd come to Georgetown. I gave him the names of all of the people I knew who might have been involved, and the descriptions of those people for whom I didn't have names. I told him what my previous companion had told me. I cautioned him she was probably in danger, and she would probably be heading back to Wisconsin very soon.

"My boss's wife is going to be pretty angry with me in the morning about that car."

Don drove me out to the airport, explained the circumstances of the damage to the previous rental and arranged for an identical car. It had to be cleaned out. We waited and talked for twenty minutes. The car was delivered to the door. He insisted on following me to the hotel, and walked me to my door. I didn't resist when he kissed me goodnight. He started to ask for more, but being a gentleman he stepped back, opened my door for me, and kissed me goodbye.

I had just gotten into my room and turned on the television to see if there was any news about the explosion when the phone rang. It was Don.

"Hello Don. Did you forget something?"

"How did you know....?"

"I'm a witch."

"I'll buy that, you've got me bewitched." There was silence while we both thought of things we wanted to say but didn't. "I forgot to ask you for your home address and telephone number, just in case I'm in the neighborhood."

I gave him the information, he said some more nice things, I resisted the temptation to ask him up again, and convinced myself it was just the uniform. After I hung up, I thought it could have been the gorgeous green eyes, or the curly black hair, or the terrific lips, or the beautiful muscles, or...the combination of those and other things. He was a dream. I fell asleep thinking about him, and dreamed of a man who was a combination of Don, Tommy, Danny and Gerry. Suddenly I was being chased by little aliens in cigar-shaped vehicles. One of them beamed me up, and I went up, up, up into the sky. I awoke smiling with the sun shining in my face, and the phone ringing. It was Ruth. I'd had about two hours worth of sleep, but I felt good.

## CHAPTER XXXIX

Ruth and the kids let themselves into the car, while I made a call to confirm my appointment with the attorney at 3:00 that afternoon. His secretary told me he'd been "unexpectedly called out of town."

I made my way to the car, lost in thought.

"What happened to the car?" asked Elizabeth.

I'm caught, I thought. "What's wrong with the car?" I asked.

"It's just different," said Elizabeth.

"There's nothing wrong with the car," said Ruth.

"Different." said Teddy.

"It does seem different," said Julia.

"It's just another rental car, like every other rental car I've ever seen," I said. That satisfied them all.

We headed South to Mount Vernon, and spent the

213

entire morning climbing hills, and hauling Ruth up some steep steps. The kids had a ball. We had to haul Teddy back under some ropes in George's bedroom. Teddy did look cute on the bed, but the guide was just a little upset with us.

We ate lunch at a nice restaurant on the grounds, bought homemade soap and packages of antique seeds from the gardens, sent some postcards back home, and drove back toward Alexandria. Just as we passed the hotel, we decided to go on to Arlington National Cemetery.

We were standing in line waiting to buy tickets for the riding tour when I noticed a child in front of us wearing a Fairview t-shirt. I introduced myself and learned the family was indeed from Fairview. In fact, the man was an acquaintance of Gerald's. He said, "It's such a shame what happened to that family, don't you think?" He cocked his head to one side in an odd way when he said it.

We commented on the smallness of the world, and talked until we reached the front of the line. I took a picture of him and his family with my cell phone camera. We scrambled to get seats on the shuttle, and sought to entertain Teddy. I lost sight of the Fairview Family. Teddy was pretty bored with a bunch of tombstones. We toured General Lee's Mansion.

214

I caught sight of the Fairview Man as I went up a stairway. He was looking at me in an odd way. I didn't see his wife or children.

Ruth and I tried to tell the kids who Audie Murphy was when we came upon his grave. There haven't been a lot of reruns, but I have this thing about short cowboys, and watch all the Alan Ladd, Audie Murphy and Roy Rogers videos I can find.

Julia and Elizabeth were properly awed by the grave of JFK, and Teddy loved the changing of the guard at the Tomb of the Unknown Soldier.

Ruth loved the view from the Tomb of the Unknown Soldier out over the Potomac with the Lincoln Memorial in the distance. It was an awesome sight.

By the time we got back to the car, Ruth and I were taking turns carrying Teddy, and the girls were getting grumpy. I was a little grumpy myself. It was time for a nap.

We got back to the hotel at 6:00 P.M. There was a note at the desk for Ruth. It was from Ralph. He wanted her to call him right away.

I excused myself and went to my room. I took a shower, and put on my pajamas and called room service.

215

There was a knock on the door. It was Ruth.

"Ralph says you blew our car up."

"How did he find out?"

"Tell me what happened."

"I didn't want you to worry."

"So fill me in."

When I'd finished telling her the story my supper arrived, and she watched me eat. Then she took the tray, tucked me in and turned off the lights.

I don't remember much after that until the phone rang about midnight. It was Don. But I was disoriented. The room was dark and I couldn't find the phone. I finally found it.

"Hi there."

"Do you always answer the phone so seductively?"

"It could be somebody really interesting on the other end."

"Did you know it was me?"

"Yes."

"Can I come over?"

"I promised to stay in tonight and be good."

"That's even more tempting."

"I should say no."

"Please."

"How soon can you be here?"

"I am here. I'm in the lobby."

"I'll be down in fifteen minutes."

In ten minutes I'd thrown on some makeup, my hair cooperated with a miracle, and I put on some cutoffs and a t-shirt.

He was waiting in the lobby. He was wearing faded jeans and a light blue t-shirt. It wasn't just the uniform that made him sexy.

As he led me into the dark bar, where we went to an even darker corner, I had the fleeting feeling we were being watched. The waitress arrived, and I ordered mineral water. He ordered a cup of coffee. As soon as she left he took my hand and held it. He looked into my eyes, asking me questions. I don't remember the questions. I don't remember my answers. I remember he stroked my hands, and looked into my eyes, and it was the most seductive thing that had ever happened to me. He didn't make any moves on me, I didn't feel I had to fight him off. I felt he was going to have to fight me off, if it were to continue much longer. I let it continue for nearly an hour. He only touched my hands. I can't call it

217

love, but it was something special.

He walked me up to my room, and kissed me goodnight at the door. While he was kissing me, I kept my hands behind my back. As he pushed the door open, he kissed me again. I took a deep breath, thanked him for a lovely evening and took another deep breath as he pushed me gently inside and pulled the door shut between us.

His last words to me were, "Don't forget the deadbolt."

"You are so stupid, Poppy Hannah!" I said to myself.

I went into the bathroom and took a hot shower, washed my hair, and turned on the television. An old romantic movie was playing. I fell asleep during a love scene.

Morning came too soon.

## CHAPTER XXXX

The wake up call was for 4:00 A.M. Ruth knocked on my door a couple of minutes later. I couldn't ignore her, so I crawled out of bed and opened the door for her.

"Why do you have that silly grin on your face?" she asked.

"I had a visitor last night."

"You didn't!"

"No. I didn't. But maybe I should have."

"Wow, Poppy. This isn't like you."

"Just a short holiday romance, is all."

"Who is he? I don't remember seeing you interested in anyone."

"He's the police officer who brought me home after the car was blown up."

219

"That is a short holiday romance...and under extremely strange circumstances, too. Tell me about it."

"We just sat in the bar and talked. He held my hand. He stroked my hand. It was the most seductively sexy thing that ever happened to me. I was ready to throw myself at him."

I must have gotten an even dopier look, because, Ruth said, "Poppy!"

"I swear he only touched my hand. He brought me up to my room, he kissed me goodbye. I locked the door and fell asleep."

"I believe you. One of you had good sense. I'm not sure it was you. That's not at all like you Poppy."

"I know. Maybe Hazel's right. Maybe it's time to start thinking about settling down." I struggled to pull a brush through my hair, as I drifted off in thought. "Nahh. It's not time to settle down yet. I'll get over it. He just showed up when my hormones were ripe or something. I'll be okay."

"Well get dressed. We have to be at the airport at 5:15."

"Meet you downstairs at 4:30."

I was downstairs with my luggage, ready to go after

Ruth to help her with hers when they all straggled down hauling their bags. As we headed toward the car, Don pulled up in a police car. He jumped out. I introduced him to Ruth.

"I thought I'd better check out this rental car before you all take off in it." he said.

He and his partner made a thorough inspection as they searched every part of the car. I tried not to notice when he bent over and looked under the car. Ruth caught me looking up at the sky, and started laughing. I started laughing, and then Don came over, grabbed me, bent me over and kissed me. Elizabeth and Julia giggled.

Teddy ran up to him and started shouting, "Let my Poppy alone you dummy." He hit at him, until Don swooped him up and sat him on top of the police car.

"Your Poppy, eh?" He gave Teddy a fierce glare. "How many other men do you have girl?" He looked at me. I hoped I didn't look as guilty as it made me feel.    "How about a police escort to the airport?" He looked at Teddy. "Would you like to ride in the police car with the siren and the lights going?"

And that's what happened. We were escorted out of town by the police, sirens and all. I got another hug and a wonderful kiss at the airport. I don't remember the flight home.      I felt guilty when Tommy met us at the airport. He was in a squad car.

Teddy asked, "Are you going to kiss Poppy, too?"

Tommy looked at me. I shrugged. Tommy kissed me hello. Then I was totally confused. He asked if he could take me out that night. I begged off.

I'd been home about ten minutes when Gerry called asking me to go to the stock car races with him. I said I'd love to go some other time.

The only man in my life not giving me attention was Mousie. He was not giving me kisses. He was ignoring me totally. I chased him into my bedroom where he hid under the bed. I couldn't figure out why he was acting so spooky.

I picked him up, hugged him, and talked to him. He purred very quietly.

I was awakened at 2:30 A.M. when he began talking. "Haarow! Haaraar-rou?"

I told him to shut up. I tried to go back to sleep, but he kept talking.

I jumped awake, on my feet. He was looking out the window. I looked out the window. There were two moving shadows in my backyard. One of the shadows was near my garage window. I crept silently to the kitchen, slid over to the door to the garage, and flipped the switch illuminating the interior of the garage. I heard noises inside, and then I heard my scrap barrel overturn. As scuffling noises ensued. I headed for the phone. There was no dial tone.

I ran back to my bedroom where I'd stupidly left my cell phone. I sneaked back to the front door trying to dial 911, but the silly phone kept flipping to another app.

## CHAPTER XXXXI

I flipped on the front porch light, looked out the window and saw what I thought might be a black Lexus racing away from the house. I opened the door, ran to Marge's house and hammered on the door. I looked back at my porch. Mousie was sitting in the kitchen door. I raced back, picked him up and ran back to Marge's. More hammering brought her husband to the door. He let me in, and Marge called the police. Tommy wasn't on duty, but a competent pair of officers arrived and made a thorough search of my house.

"Is there anything in your garage anyone would want to steal?" I was asked.

"I don't really know. There's a lot of stuff out there. I try to keep space so I can put my car in when the weather is bad. I don't know what's there."

"Can you tell if anything is missing."

225

"It's just a lot messier than it was before.  I'll have to ask Hazel to come over and look it over and see if anything is missing."  Then I spied a cigar box sitting on top of the garage door opener.  I pointed to it.  "I think they added something instead of taking something away."

One of the officers raced for his car, the other escorted me outside, pointed me toward Marge.  She was holding Mousie.  Meanwhile the other officer got a wrench from the trunk of his car and went around the side of the house to turn off the gas.

Within twenty minutes the bomb squad had removed the cigar box from atop the garage door opener.

I fell asleep in Marge's spare room with Mousie curled up next to me. While I slept the bomb squad went over my house looking for other bombs.

Marge awakened me about an hour later. Tommy was there, and so was Ralph.  I had an idea  my present appearance would frighten them both, but I had nothing with which to repair the damage.  They'd have to see me looking like Bozo gone Berserk.  It had to happen sometime, I guess.

"What do I have to do, ship you to Timbuktu?"  asked Ralph.

226

"Did you know Timbuktu had one of the earliest centers for the study of law? It was founded in the year 1100. It's in Mali, near the Sahara. I'd love to go there sometime." I said.

"Don't try changing the subject on me, young lady! And how do you <u>know</u> all of these things!?" He seemed more than a little exasperated with me, so I made an imaginary key, and sealed my lips.

Then Tommy started on me. He threatened to move in. Then he tried to put his arm around me. I was holding Mousie and Mousie took a swipe at him, as if to tell him to leave me alone.     "I'm really sleepy guys. And I didn't invite those people to put a bomb in my garage. Can I go to sleep? I'll let you yell at me in the morning."

"You're going to be in the office in the morning?" asked Ralph.

"I promise." He backed off when I said that. Tommy patted me on the shoulder, and then he patted Mousie. Mousie still loved him. I was still confused about who to love.

# CHAPTER XXXXII

The next morning dawned bright and blue with cotton puff clouds dotting the western horizon. Maybe it would stay that way until I got back from Fairview tonight. I was beginning not to be too fond of rainy nights in Fairview, and I was still somewhat wary of driving alone at night after the kidnaping, the car bombing and the break-ins at my house. But then I'm either fearless or just plain foolish. I remembered all of the close calls, and decided I wasn't fearless. That leaves foolish. I went anyway as soon as I got off work.

As I pulled into Fairview and drove into the gas station, I was waiting for Blackie to roll out his battery charger. I wanted to tell him I didn't need a battery charge. Somehow, he already knew I didn't need it. He strolled out to the car with a question in his eyes.

"Can I help you?"

229

"Well, I was going to tell you I didn't need a boost, but I guess you already know."

"Oh, well. I, uh... I guess I figured you'd had it fixed by now."

"What kind of batteries do you sell in your station?"

"Well, I've got several kinds."

"What one would you put in your car, if you were choosing?"

"Why are you asking all of these questions?"

"Why are you answering me with a question?"

"I guess I don't like where this is leading."

"Do you have anything to feel guilty about?"

"No. Why should I?"

"There you go again answering with a question. Do you know Tom's Wrecker Service?"

"Yeah, I know Tom. We've got an agreement where he drags cars in here if they need fixing."

"Do you know where I could find Tom?"

"What for?"

"I need to talk to him."

"Why'd you want to do that?"

"I almost think you've got something to hide here. Why

do you keep answering me with more questions?"

"I've got nothing to hide. Tom's place is down this street, and through the first alley to your right. Go all the way to the end of the alley, and you'll see his wrecker there."

He started to walk away, then turned and said, "I heard you met my daughter, Marianne?"

"Yeah, she helped me understand some things...and so have you."

"Try to keep her out of it. She didn't have anything to do with Gerald's death." he said.

"Thanks...for everything."

## CHAPTER XXXXIII

At first, the wrecker owner tried to keep the mystery going, but he caved in pretty fast when I pointed to the wrecker and told him I'd seen it pulling my car away from the abandoned farm house. He broke down and reluctantly admitted Norm Summerfield had called him to come and drag my car in to Blackie's station. He rolled it into the station and fixed it himself. It needed a new distributor cap.

"The old one crumbled right in my hand."

I decided my luck was holding just long enough with all of this probing. I drove past Norm Summerfield's gun shop and saw him stop as he walked past the door and stare out at my car. Just as abruptly he pulled down the shade over the door, and the lights inside went out. Rather than pressing my luck any further I decided to put my visit with Norm off to another day. I still had a couple of things I wanted to check

233

out.

On the way out of town I ran into Gerry. He was driving a restored red and white 1957 Bellaire convertible. He motioned for me to pull over to the side of the road, so I pulled into the drive-in and shut off my engine. He jumped out of the car and climbed into my passenger seat.

"I just wanted to let you know what a great time I had on our date."

"I had a nice time, too."

"I tried to call you all last weekend and all I got was your machine."

"I'm sorry I missed you."

Gerry put his arm behind my headrest, and leaned closer to me. "I really like you a lot. Could we go out again."

"I'm still trying to help Danny." I said, changing the direction of the conversation. "Do you suppose you could answer some questions for me?"

"Sure, anything."

"Did you and Danny have a fight about something just after his mother was killed?"

"Yeah, but it was nothing."

"What happened?"

"He was pretty bummed out, I guess.  He called me Junior, and it pissed me off.  I don't like being called Junior...makes me sound like a kid.  It doesn't matter any more, cause now I'm the Gerald Rivers.  Not gonna be 'Junior' anymore."  The remembered rage oozed out of his pores.

I changed the subject.  "Do you have any idea who might have killed Shorty?"

"Nah, he probably blew himself up lighting a match in there or something."

"Is that your car?" I asked.  "I've seen you driving sixteen different vehicles since I met you."

"Sixteen?  Naah.  I don't think so.  I help out a friend that owns a car lot in Collington.  He lets me drive his cars is all."

"What did your father look like, Gerry?"

"I don't know.  People say I look just like him.  I can't see it.  I guess we're built pretty much the same.  Same height and all.  But I'm not anything like him otherwise.  Why?"

"Just wondering."  I moved away from him as he reached for my hand.

He twisted around in the seat, and looked at me, lowering his head so that he looked through his lashes like a

235

puppy dog. He knew the tricks all right. "What's the score here? Are you dating someone else?"

"I haven't made any serious commitments to anyone, Gerry."

"Then will you go out with me again this weekend."

I begged off, saying I had a lot of work to catch up on because I'd been away last weekend and "tied up" before I left. I watched him carefully trying to decide if he'd been in on the kidnaping, at the same time trying to see if I could see any evidence of drug abuse. I couldn't tell one way or the other. He just seemed to be angry I wasn't going out with him again.

## CHAPTER XXXXIV

I couldn't wait to get off work the next night. I had to fend off Ruth's invitation for more soup, and my mother called me at work, because I hadn't checked in for such a long time. I had one on each line, and when I told Ruth my mother was on the other line, she muttered something about keeping in touch. That's the last thing I need, Ralph on my case again.

After I'd talked to my mother and changed into Levi's and a sweatshirt, I drove to Fairview. It was still light when I pulled up in front of Norm Summerfield's gun shop. Norm saw me coming and headed for the door, but I had it open and was inside before he could stop me. He scowled.

I gave him my surprised and hurt look. I hoped it passed for innocence that would disarm him. I think it just

237

confused him.   At any rate, I hurried to ask him some questions, before he could throw me out.

"What do you know about Danny Johnson and his mother."

"Why ask me?"

"Is there some kind of disease around here that causes everyone to answer questions with questions."

"Huh?

"There you go again."

Norm sort of jumped as a car went by the window, then hurried past me, pulled down the shade and locked the door.

I picked up a rifle that was lying on the counter and feigned interest and/or intelligence in the product.

"Did you sell Danny his 30.06?"

"Yeah, I did."

"Who'd you tell about it?"

"Can't recall as I told anyone."

"Did you know Guy was in love with Alice?"

"Everybody knew that."

"Do you think Guy shot Rivers?"

"I don't care who shot him."

I placed the rifle carefully on the glass counter top

pointing away from Norm. He picked it up and locked it into a rack behind the counter. I climbed onto a saddle that was perched on a saw horse, and placing my chin in my hands, rested my elbows on the glass counter. Norm relaxed.

"So why'd you run me off the road and kidnap me?"

Norm jumped and looked around. I don't know whether he thought I was wired, or somebody was in the back room listening or what, but he was pretty nervous. Affecting innocence himself, in a gruff voice, he said, "Didn't do neither."

"Well, thanks for fixing my car. It needed it."

He didn't answer, but seemed to relax again.

"Do you think Guy killed Rivers?"

"He's my brother. He had reason."

"Do you think he did it?"

"I don't know. He was really mad at me for running you off the road. You were nosing around too much. I was afraid of what you'd find."

"Do you have something to hide?"

"It ain't' no secret what I thought of Rivers. He was losing me business. Nobody could get a gun permit. I told half the town I was going to kill him for it."

"Did you?

"No. I sort of wish I'd had the guts to do it, though. Guy really loved Alice. He's been really hurting since Rivers killed her."

"Do you know anything about the explosion at the feed mill?"

"Only that Shorty died in the explosion. Figure he lit something he shouldn't have."

"Ever heard of a bean bomb?"

Norm looked at me as if I'd flipped out. I figured he was about ready to throw me out the door, so I hurried to fill him in. "You checked out an Army publication on Booby Traps from the library."

"Did I? You are a snoopy little thing! I read all sorts of army books. We've got us a little survival group that gets together."

I quickly switched subjects again. "How easy would it be to switch rifle barrels?"

Norm was confused, and didn't answer, trying to figure out what my next move was going to be, then he asked, "What you getting at?"

"Well, if the rifling on the bullet that killed Rivers came

from a certain barrel, could that barrel have come off one gun, then be switched to another rifle just like it?"

"You mean to Danny's rifle? Nah, I don't think anybody'd do that." Suddenly he had a far off gaze, as if he were remembering something from the past.

My last question before I left was "Have you switched any barrels on 30.06 rifles lately, or has anyone ordered new ones?"

"I haven't, but maybe...maybe one of the other guys has. I'll have to look that up in my records." He said it a little late, as if he'd stopped himself in the middle of a thought. He walked to the door, unlocked it and stood until I walked out.

As I walked away, I took a picture of the white Cadillac with my cell phone.

## CHAPTER XXXXV

The next day was not memorable, though it was probably the closest I ever get to normal. The highlight of the day was when Ruth came to use the phone in the library to talk to a friend. I was in my office, and Ralph was down the hall in his. I answered the phone, put it on hold, and rather than using the intercom, I shouted to Ralph, "Mr. Gerken is on line one."

Ruth shouted from the library, "What's the matter is he in a pickle?"

Ralph joined in from his office when he called out, "Come on you guys, that's not kosher."

That's as exciting as it got all day, though it was good for a laugh.

In order to spice up the day, I went to see Danny at the jail. I'd left my purse and my paralegal bar card at work, but I

243

waved some papers at the desk guard who must have assumed I was delivering papers from an attorney.

He let me in to talk to Danny, and left.

"Are you still working on this?" Danny asked.

"As much as I can."

"Isn't kidnaping and car bombing enough to make you quit?"

"I've got new information."

I told Danny about the bean bomb. He acted as if he thought I'd lost my marbles. What's so darn weird about a bean bomb?

"Would it be possible to switch barrels on a rifle?" I asked.

He shrugged. I thought I saw a glint of excitement in his eyes, but it melted so fast I couldn't be sure.

He should have been excited about the question. Entertained some possibilities. I thought he'd jump at the idea, but he didn't want to talk about it. In fact, he didn't want to talk to me about anything. I left thoroughly discouraged, but I tried not to let on to Danny. On the way out to the car, I decided to check my theory out with a gunsmith in the city. My car started immediately.

244

"Thank you Norm, thank you Tony-Tom."

The local gunsmith told me about gun barrels. Again, more than I ever wanted to know about gun barrels and rifling. If the question ever comes up on Trivial Pursuit, I'll have the answers. I know a lot of trivial things. Sometimes it does pay off.

He told me about firing pins, and the marks they leave behind on the brass. I think he was getting a little tired of my dumb questions, but he kept right on answering them, and in the process I learned a great deal about rifling, as well as the effects of switching rifle barrels. It was a definite possibility.

While I was sitting there, I took a picture of his business card and emailed it to my office address. He might make a good witness if we needed one. I had already taken pictures, made notes and printed them all out and pasted them on 3x5 cards. They were my clue cards. I used them to "think outside the box".

My first rule is: don't ask if there are rules, someone will make one up for you.

## CHAPTER XXXXVI

Later, I was sitting, once again sifting through my clue cards, when I remembered Margaret Lafferty. I'd been kidnaped the weekend I'd meant to go see her, then the trip to Washington interfered. I rummaged through my notes and found her number. I gave her a call.

She said, "I've really got to talk to you. There's something you need to know...No! I don't buy anything hawked by telephone."

I held the phone away from my ear and peered at it, as if to see the answer to the conversation that had just ensued. As soon as she'd ended her sentence she had slammed the telephone down, disconnecting us.

I went to see Danny again. He was still not answering my questions directly. Still avoiding my eyes.

"Look, don't worry about me. I'll be fine."

"You keep getting into trouble. Your boss said if

247

anything happened to you because of me, he wouldn't defend me."

"He likes to think he's got this power over me. Don't mind him. He doesn't really mean it."

"But you could have been hurt bad."

"I wasn't. In fact, I'm better off now than I was before. Come on, just tell me all you can remember, okay?"

Danny still wouldn't look me in the eyes, but he shrugged, and his body language said he wanted to talk, so I kept prying.

Finally he just blurted out, "Guy really loved Mom. He's always been good to me."

It startled me. Then I had a revelation. "Do you think Guy killed your step-father?"

"Yeah, he must have. He hated him as much as I did, and he loved Mom. We were the only ones with motives."

"I don't understand."

"I <u>know</u> I didn't kill him. It had to be Guy."

"That's exactly what Guy said," I told him. And the hard part was, I believed both of them.

"Why didn't you tell me earlier." I asked.

"He loved Mom. I didn't want to hurt him."

248

"What made you change your mind?

"I don't like sitting in jail." He said.

"I've been told it's not the greatest thing in the world."

"The noise is the worst thing. It's never quiet." Danny looked around him. It was relatively quiet in the interview room.

"Danny, tell me about your relationship with Gerry."

"We were always good friends, up until the last, and then, just before Mom died, Gerry started acting funny."

"How funny?"

"He just cooled off. Wouldn't talk to me. Probably from the things his Dad was saying about him."

"What did he say."

"He was always putting him down. It made me feel sort of funny because he'd point to me, and say, 'Why can't you be more of a man, like Dan' then Gerry would really lose it."

"What do you mean, 'lose it?'" I asked.

"He'd lose his temper. And when he didn't lose his temper he'd look like he was about to explode. Gerald was always calling him a sissy, and even called him a fag a couple of times."

"Do you know if Gerry was into drugs?" I asked.

249

"Yeah, he did that, too.  He said he'd quit.  But I was never sure he did.  He was really good at covering it up."

"Do you know who his suppliers were?" I asked.

"I met a couple of them.  They change from time to time."

"I've been told Gerald busted up a drug ring in Washington, D.C. by accident.  Do you know anything about that?"

"I don't know how much of an accident it was.  I think Gerald was trying to get Gerry out of trouble and stumbled onto something.

## CHAPTER XXXXVII

I went back to the office and tried to get some work done. I should have sailed right through it. Ralph was out of the office and the receptionist was getting all of the calls. I couldn't concentrate on it, but I struggled through. About halfway into a very boring transcription tape, I decided to take a break.

I pulled out some colored index cards and began writing down what I knew so far about Gerald Rivers, about Alice Rivers, about Gerry, about Danny, Norm, Guy, Tom's Wrecker Service, Annie and Shorty. While I was working Kara came in and placed a large envelope on my desk and said something about discovery. I didn't pay any attention.

I shuffled them together with my clue cards, and then I went through the cards every way from Sunday, I added cards for all of the other people I'd talked to, and still didn't get anywhere with it. I went into the library and sat on the floor and spread them all out and looked at them from six different directions. Finally, I gathered them all up and threw them up in the air, and looked at them out of the corner of my eye to see if I could see anything I'd missed. It still looked like big pieces of confetti with absolutely no meaning.

I tried spacing out. I tried "asking my angels" the way Hazel does it. A persistent little voice kept giving me the same answer, but it didn't make any sense. I pushed it aside and went back to look at the cards again. Nothing.

I gathered up my mess, and went back out to my office to try assembling everything on the computer to see if it made any more sense. I was shocked to find it was dark outside. I looked at the clock in the waiting room. It was a little after eight. Suddenly my stomach took note of the time and began snarling like a tiger. "Shut up. I'll feed you later."

I got a sugar-free ginger ale out of the refrigerator, took it back to the waiting room and settled onto the couch, putting my feet up. I jumped up, went to the door, locked it, and went back and settled down again.

Maybe this new environment would clear out my

senses. The tiger in my tank growled louder. I got up and rummaged through the receptionist's desk, looking for food.

Just as I was stealing Kara's last Butterfinger, the phone rang. I jumped. How did he know I was here? Maybe he didn't. Maybe he was just checking. I let it ring.

I felt guilty as I took a bite out of Kara's candy bar. Thinking about Kara made me remember what she'd said when she came into my office. She'd said, "Here's the Johnson Discovery. I'm going home." I jumped up and ran back to my office and grabbed the envelope. Maybe the police or the prosecutor had found something I didn't know about to shed some light on things.

I sat and read their probable cause affidavit. I read Danny's intake statement. I read the reports of the detectives who questioned him. There wasn't much there of which I wasn't already aware. I learned Danny had no previous record. I learned Danny's birthday was September 12, and we were about the same age. I learned he had two sisters. One lived in the next town South of Fairview, and the other, Vicky lived in California. His mother was talking on the phone to Vicky when she was killed, according to Hazel.

I looked for the autopsy report on Gerald Rivers. I

253

pulled out what I thought would be his report, and discovered they'd also sent along the autopsy report on Alice Rivers. The photographs tried to come out of the envelope with the reports. I stuffed them back in. I didn't need to look at those now, if ever. Particularly not when I was alone in an office building downtown in the middle of the night.

My heart jumped into my throat as the clock behind me suddenly began chiming. It was only nine o'clock. I was getting very hungry. I went back and rummaged through my desk drawer looking for change. I discovered the bullets from the Derringer, and stuck them in my pocket. I retrieved the gun itself from under my envelopes. I fished a cartridge out and loaded the gun, and slipped it into the pocket of my blazer. Why was I arming myself? "If you're scared, why don't you just stay up here until you're ready to go home?" I asked myself.

I shouldn't have even thought about looking at those autopsy pictures. The thought brought back a vision of a previous autopsy picture. A bullet to the head. For purposes of the autopsy, the head had been removed from the body. The photo of the body looked like a turkey ready for stuffing. I shivered in revulsion at the memory of the sight. My stomach growled in reply.

"Shut up. How could you be hungry after remembering that awful picture?"

It growled again, as if to remind me it didn't see the picture, and it was still hungry.

I picked a couple dollars worth of change out of my desk drawer and put it in the pocket with the Derringer. I grabbed the keys off my desk and left the office, locking the door. As I turned to walk down the hall, I heard a sound behind me. I couldn't be sure, but I thought the door to the stairs at the East end of the hallway had moved just a hair. The sounds I'd heard seemed to have come from the same place. Now there was absolutely no sound at all. There was another stairwell at the other end of the hall, and this hallway was crossed by a shorter one that contained the elevators. It was probably only the cleaning people. I walked to the elevators. Before I had a chance to push the button, I heard an elevator motor engage. I could hear it approaching and just when I thought it would arrive at my floor, I heard the bell ringing for the floor above. The doors opened and closed above me.

I stepped back around the corner from the elevator shaft, and waited until the elevator door opened. I waited. I heard someone inside clear their throat. Probably just a cleaning person. However, it was only eight floors down, and I was spooked.

The building was thirteen stories high, but the elevator only goes to twelve. It's a solid, rectangular style, built for function rather than beauty. The only concessions to design were the brass and marble in the lobby. It had been a bank at one time, and had been converted to an office building. The management had put in new windows that didn't open, but failed to revamp the heating and cooling system, leaving a certain stuffiness in the air. The stairwell at the other end of the building leads outside to an alleyway, sometimes inhabited by homeless alcoholics, who live in the dumpster. They've been known to hide out in the building in the winter, and I've seen their wet barefoot prints coming out of the restroom. I decided to take the stairs at this end of the building.

The soda and candy machines were in an alcove in the basement, just around the corner from the stairway. As I opened the stairway door, I held my breath and listened. I didn't hear a thing. The elevator was no longer moving either.

I ran down to the next landing, my footsteps echoing all the way from the top to the bottom and back again. I stopped, held my breath and listened again. I did this at each landing, both for my peace of mind, and because I was getting tired. I would definitely take the elevator back up. Or I would leave the lights burning all night and run out to my car and hurry home, lock all the doors, jump in bed and pull the covers over my head, making sure to keep my back to the wall all the way there, so the ghosts and spooks and scary things wouldn't get me.

"Wait a minute!" I mentally shouted to myself. "You're scared of ghosts for heavens sake!"

"Yeah," I answered back just as silently. I ran the rest of the way down the stairs to the basement bravely, with my hand in my pocket cradling the Derringer. I realized I'd left my cell phone lying on my desk. I'd have to go back to the office. The phone was my alarm clock!

In the basement, I chose a bag of microwave popping corn, punched the proper number on the machine, grabbed the bag out of the machine, and ran back to the elevator. I punched a button, and I heard the elevator start from just above me. The doors flew open. There was no one inside. I punched the basement button and the eight, hoping it would by-pass all of other floors and take me directly to my floor

257

without stopping. I held my breath as it raced to the eighth floor.

I stepped off the elevator, popcorn under my arm, the Derringer in my right hand, and the key to the door in my left hand. Just as I rounded the corner, I saw a figure wearing black disappear through the stairwell door at the end of the corridor. I ran down the hall, my back to the wall, and unlocked the office door, jumped inside and pushed the door shut. It locked reassuringly. I jumped as the phone rang. It was Hazel.

"Hi, I'm sure glad you called Hazel."

"Why are you still there?"

"I've been going over the discovery, looking for clues."

"Why don't you bring it home with you, and I'll come over and fix you something to eat."

"That's a great idea. Except someone is stalking me."

"Call Tommy. Right now." She said.

I did. He wasn't there. The dispatcher promised to have someone there in fifteen minutes.

Fifteen minutes later, no one had arrived. I punched in the police desk number on my cell phone and set it for quick dial, grabbed my index cards, pulled everything but the photos

258

out of the prosecutor's envelope, and slipped it all into my tote bag, grabbed my purse and ran out the door. I left the lights on. I ran down the hallway with my back to the wall, my eyes on the door at the end of the corridor.

I called the elevator and it opened as if it had been waiting for me. I jumped in pushed "one" and the elevator dropped to the main floor. Behind me I heard the other elevator start up. I ran to the front door, fumbling with the lock, finally shoved the door open and ran for my car. I jumped in forgetting to turn off my car alarm. I was out on the street headed for home when the alarm went off. I stopped in the middle of the street and turned it off. So much for making an inconspicuous retreat. As I started up again, I saw a black Lexus, with darkened windows pull out into the street from the same parking lot I'd just left. It followed me all the way home. I pulled into my driveway, and it sped past. I ran to the side door, forgetting to set my car alarm. The house was dark. I flipped on all of the lights, and locked the doors. I ran around the house checking all of the doors and windows, closing blinds and pulling curtains over them. I even went so far as to pin my living room drapes shut, because they wouldn't hang straight and there was a gap through which a mouse might have peered at me. Just then my Mouse came up behind me and rubbed against my legs. He jumped up to the window and stuck his nose through the curtain where I'd just pinned it shut. I picked him up and hugged him, and put the curtain back.

I was busy rechecking all of my security when I heard a sound in the driveway. Belatedly I remembered the gun I'd taken from the office safe was in the trunk of my car. Or maybe it wasn't there anymore. I hadn't seen it since before I'd been kidnaped and my car had been stolen. The baby Derringer was in my pocket. I loaded it with one bullet. It didn't instill confidence.

Mousie was standing at the window, saying "Haaarrrroww. Haaarow-yow?"

I ran to the basement and rummaged through sports equipment. I grabbed a tennis racket and a croquet mallet. As I turned off the basement light, I saw a shadow flit across in front of the basement window next to the driveway. I quietly sneaked up the basement stairs, I heard footsteps on my porch. Then I heard something heavy drop onto the floor of the porch. I reached carefully around the basement door to the side door and simultaneously flipped off the kitchen lights as I turned on the porch light.

Suddenly something brushed across my face. I dropped the baby Derringer on the floor. It fired. I screamed. There was heavy knocking on the door, and I heard a voice screaming.

"Poppy. Poppy. Let us in."

It was Hazel. I flipped the kitchen light back on, knocked the cat off the cupboard where he was, once again, trying to flick his tail into my face, and unlocked the back door to let Hazel in the house. Tommy was right behind her.

"What's going on here? The very last thing you were told was to stay put. Who fired a shot?" Tommy was steaming. He saw the baby Derringer on the floor, picked it up and snorted. "You call this protection?!" He snorted again. He stomped off through the house opening closet doors and slamming them again.

"What's going on here?" asked Hazel. She was inspecting the bullet hole in the ceiling of the kitchen.

"I have been letting my imagination get away from me. I got myself spooked. I'll try not to let it happen again."

I helped Hazel carry her stuff in, including the large pot she'd dropped on the floor of the porch which, it turns out was filled with potato salad. As I turned back to pull the door shut,

261

I saw the black Lexus crawl by the house. As it sped away, I noticed it had California plates.

I called to Tommy, and he raced out the door, rushed back, kissed me and left with instructions to lock everything up.

Hazel cooked up a vegetarian taco salad, as I went through the various reports. One of the discovery items was a report from a man named John Ivy. The report didn't say why he'd made this report, or who he was with. But it contained very interesting information about Gerry Rivers.

I'd never thought to ask Gerry what he did for a living. Apparently Mr. Ivy was wondering what Gerry did for a living, and was investigating him. He didn't appear to have any concrete evidence, but he had a lot of conjectures about his activities.

"Hey Hazel. Ask your guides what Gerry Rivers does for a living."

"Okay, let me work on it." She was chopping tomatoes and throwing them into a bowl atop lettuce.

"Did you get anything?"

"It doesn't relate to anything I know."

"What does it look like?"

"Well, a kitchen?"

262

"Is he a chef?"

"No. Not a chef. That doesn't feel right."

"Maybe he's a chemist."

"What makes you think he's a chemist?"

"I don't know. I don't think that's right either."

"So what's he doing?"

"Counting money in a kitchen."

"Maybe he's a banker."

"Nope that doesn't seem right either. Let me think on this. I can't figure it out. It's not your ordinary nine to five job."

I made a list of all of the witnesses I wanted to speak to personally from the prosecutor's witness list, and added a couple of names of my own. I'd already talked to Marianne Rupley and Danny's sister. I still wanted to talk to other neighbors of Alice, and in particular I wanted to speak to the head of the State Police Recruiter who had recommended Danny for admittance to their training program.

****

The next day was uneventful. I did some long-neglected gardening, took a shower, fixed myself a light lunch and pulled out my notes to study them. I went through the clue cards again, and sorted everything having to do with Gerry

Rivers. I wondered if he was still using cocaine. We'd had clients who were users, but I'd never been able to figure out the signs. Ralph said they couldn't keep a story straight, and they stumbled over their words and were pretty irrational when they were due to score, but he said they usually seemed pretty normal right after using the stuff. Kara wondered about people from time to time, but I didn't like to accuse anyone of using drugs, just because they were unusual. I wouldn't want anyone to accuse me of being a drug user, just because I am eccentric on occasion.

Ironically just as I finished going through all of the cards, Gerry called me. He wanted me to go out with him that night. I'd already made a date with Tommy. I picked up the phone.

## CHAPTER XXXXVIII

"Hi, Gerry."

"You really do know who's on the phone when it rings?"

"Well, I guess I do most of the time."

"That must be a great talent. If you don't want to talk to someone you don't have to answer."

"Yeah, that's a plus."

"Have you ever done that to me, Poppy?"

"Not that I recall. Usually, I only do it to my mother. It gives me a chance to do whatever she's going to nag me about before she gets the chance to nag about it!"

"Do you know why I called?"

"Well, probably."

"Would you like to go to a movie with me tonight?"

"I can't. I've already made other plans."

"Who are you going out with?"

"Just an old friend," I said.

265

"Are you sure you won't change your mind?" he asked.

"It wouldn't be fair to do that, Gerry."

"I suppose not.  But can we go out Sunday night?"

"Let's just wait and see how things go, okay?"

I hate possessiveness.  It was so thick in the things Gerry said.  I got the idea Gerry was trying to prove he was a man, in the way he dressed, the way he talked, the dates, and all.  He was a gentleman most of the time, but he would suddenly become irrational.  That bothered me.  I wasn't sure of the cause.

I'd hung up the phone and was daydreaming when it rang again.  It was Tommy.  He was going to be late.

"Hi, Tommy.  How soon will you be here?"

"Poppy?  You're doing it again.  How did you know it was me?  How do you know I'm going to be late?  What else do you know?"

"Lots of things."

"Do you know all of the lecherous things I think about you?"

"Probably."

"And you still talk to me.  You're amazingly tolerant!"

"Maybe I think lecherous thoughts about you, too."

266

"Actions speak louder than words."

"Who's talking?"

"Love is a participant sport, Poppy."

"You've told me that before, too."

"Well, I never give up. I'm going to be late, as you know. Do you also know the reason I'm late is we're working on a big drug deal? I'm afraid to even think about it around you! Don't mention a word of this to anyone, you hear?"

"You're the one that mentioned it. I didn't hear a thing!"

"I'm getting paranoid. It's big and exciting. I'm sorry I can't say more."

"I know," I said. I had an idea it was very big and very exciting. I wished I could pump him for more information, but my usual nosy self kept quiet.

"I have to go home and get cleaned up. I won't be there until about eleven. Can we go out for a pizza and then watch a pay-per-view movie or something?"

"Sounds great."

I glanced out the window as I hung up the phone. Gerry's little black pickup truck went by. Well, it's a free country. I guess I can't stop him from checking up on me, I thought.

## CHAPTER  XXXXIX

Tommy didn't get to my house until about 11:45. Someone had called him from work with some more information. He didn't say what it was, but apparently it was important for him to get it right away. I didn't ask.

He walked in the door with flowers behind his back. As he presented them with a flourish, I recognized they were just like the zinnias I had planted next to my garage. They look wonderful outside. They smell terrible inside. I exclaimed over them and popped them into a vase, and set them in the kitchen window, where I told him, everyone could see them. Privately, I put them in the window so they could at least see outside. I think they like it better outside, and that's why they smell so bad when you bring them in. They haven't told me, but I suspect it's so.

As I grabbed my purse to leave, he confessed he'd

269

picked them from beside my garage.

Tommy drives an old, nicely preserved, BMW. He likes it because it didn't cost him much, and his married co-workers think he can afford a BMW because he's single. He confesses he got a good deal, and he keeps it in good condition by spending all of his spare time on it. He looks at me accusingly when he says this. As if it's my fault he has so much free time.

We were sitting at a table, drinking soft drinks, waiting for our pizza to arrive, when I looked out the restaurant window and saw Gerry's black pickup truck sitting in the drive outside. I twisted around in my seat to see if he was in the restaurant, but couldn't find him. A few minutes later I looked back to the drive and the truck was gone.

On the way home, I thought I caught sight of the black pickup truck once again. We were in light traffic, and I glanced into the side mirror and saw it swerve to the right, and then just as quickly disappear.

When we pulled into my driveway at a quarter to one in the morning, Gerry was sitting on my front steps. His pickup truck was parked on the street. He'd been drinking. He came toward me screaming unintelligibly.

"What do you mean going out on me!" were the first

words I could make out.

Tommy stepped between us as Gerry tried to grab at me.

"Just sober up and go on home, buddy." Said Tommy. Gerry swung at Tommy, who held up an arm and fended him off. Gerry pushed at me, but I was too far away. He stumbled, and sat on the ground and began crying. Tommy turned in disgust, then bent down to help him up.

"Leave now, or I'm arresting you," said Tommy.

Gerry climbed to his feet and punched at Tommy, but missed. Tommy grabbed Gerry and shook him. Gerry pulled away, whirled toward me and shouted, "You two-timing bitch. Who do you think you are? You aren't to see any one else. Do you hear me? You will do as I say!"

"Tommy, he doesn't know what he's doing. Just get him out of here. Gerry. Please leave before you get in trouble." I shouted at Tommy, but lowered my voice to speak to Gerry, hoping he would calm down to listen.

"You're trying to ruin me." Gerry shouted.

"You aren't making any sense, Gerry." I tried to stay calm, as he hurled obscenities at me.

Tommy grabbed both of Gerry's arms from behind, and

pulled them back. He lifted Gerry off his feet, Gerry tried to kick at me, and then tried to kick at Tommy. He bent his head, trying to bite him. Tommy struggled to drag Gerry toward his pickup truck. I could hear him speaking to him as he did so. I couldn't make out what he said. Gerry seemed to calm himself.

Tommy stuffed Gerry into the driver's seat of his car, said something to him, and then slammed the door. As Tommy walked back toward me, I saw Gerry slump over the wheel. I watched to make sure he was all right. Then I saw him reach over to the glove compartment, the interior of the car lit up. I was afraid he might have a gun. Instead, he disappeared from sight. I was looking worried. Tommy glanced back at him from where he stood, shook his head and shrugged in disgust.

"He's snorting coke," he said, shaking his head. "He's lost all his sense. He knows I'm a cop."

"Are you going to arrest him?" I asked.

"No. Let's go watch that movie." He picked the pizza box off the ground where it had dropped, and we walked to the porch. We watched as Gerry calmly pulled away. He made a u-turn at the corner, and came back past the house, waving at us like we were the best of friends. As the street light illuminated his face, I could see his smile. The quickness of the change in his demeanor frightened me. It was as if someone had changed channels and we were watching a different story.

I turned to Tommy, still in awe of the complete change. "How can that happen?" I asked.

"Cocaine. I've learned a lot about it. It's more monstrous than most realize. It grabs good people and won't let them go. It fools them into believing that no one notices. They think it's their dirty little secret, but everyone knows, sooner or later." He put his arm around me and guided me into the house.

## CHAPTER XXXXIX

On the following day, Sunday, I slept in. Tommy had left about 3:00 a.m.

I set off for Fairview again. Hoping I wouldn't run into Gerry. I wanted to talk to more of the neighbors. I figured I'd have better luck on a Sunday afternoon. I interviewed everyone on the street I'd missed before. The biggest thing everyone had noticed is how sincerely they believed Gerald's grief over Alice's death. They couldn't understand how he could grieve so when he had shot her in self-defense. One wondered how anyone could hate someone enough to kill them, and then turn around and grieve them.

After talking to the neighbors I went to see the new town marshal, Everett Meadows. One of the neighbors had suggested him as a suspect because he wanted Gerald's job.

I asked him what he knew about Gerald and Alice, and

275

their deaths.

"There was a lot more there than is public knowledge," he hinted.

"Can you elaborate?"

"Well, I don't like to speak ill of the dead, but there's a lot of questions about Gerald's involvement in some drug deals that were going down."

"When did you come upon this knowledge?" I asked.

"Well, just recently."

"Is there concrete proof of this, or is this just conjecture?"

"Well, I can't say for sure. I don't have any evidence, but there's rumors. There's a lot going on in the county in the way of a big drug investigation, too."

"Has anyone said for sure that Gerald was involved?"

"Not really, but I just figured from the little bit I'd heard, and from some of the questions I've been asked about him."

"Who's been asking these questions?"

"Well there was this big shot from the D.E.A. that was here. He came to talk to me particularly." He bragged.

"Do you have any other suspicions about Gerald's behavior, or about his wife?"

276

"Well, then there's the missing money from the town clerk's office."

"Has there been an audit?" I asked.

"Well, no, I don't think so. Maybe there has. It's been talked about. I wouldn't be surprised if there was one."

"So there's no evidence that Gerald was stealing money from the town either?"

"No, not really. But who else could it a been?" he asked. I felt he was lying to me. He didn't make a lot of sense. Maybe he was just trying to keep information from me.

Meadows had a lot of questions himself, but hadn't come up with any answers. He wasn't a lot of help, but he did give me an idea of how many rumors were flying around Fairview.

## CHAPTER XXXXX

As I raced up the back steps I stumbled over a package. I kicked it aside, as I fumbled with the keys. I unlocked the door, flipped on the light, and kicked the package inside with me. It was about a foot square, and not too heavy. The phone rang. It was Gerry. I didn't answer it. I let the answering machine pick it up.

"Come on Poppy, I know you're there. Pick it up."

I ignored the voice, and kicked the package under the kitchen table. There was something about it I didn't like. I should have been very wary of strange packages after the garage bomb. But then I got side-tracked by the phone.

"Come on Poppy. Pick up."

Why did he want to talk to me?

"I'm not a druggie, Poppy."

Couldn't prove it by me. Now that I've seen a druggie, I know one when I see one. I know one who looks like he

279

wants to kill me.

"Come on Poppy. I'm..."  The machine beeped.  It'd heard enough.  So had I.

I kicked the package back out from under the table.  There was no postage and no return address.  I opened the side door to the garage, kicked it into the garage, slammed the door and locked it.  It could wait.  It had survived a lot of kicking around.

The phone rang again.  It wasn't Gerry.  I had an inkling of who it was, but I wasn't sure.  I'd only heard from him once before.  I picked it up and said hello.

"This is Harold Rivers, Poppy.  I've got some new information I thought I should share with you.  Can you meet me somewhere this evening?"

"What sort of information Mr. Rivers?"

"I'd rather not discuss it on the phone, but it'd shed some light on Gerald's murder.  I believe I can give you clear evidence that Danny Johnson had nothing to do with it."

"That's great.  Would you like to meet somewhere in Fairview?"

"No, I'd rather no one there knew I was in town.  Could you meet me at your city airport?"

"Sure, I could manage that."

"I'll be renting a Cadillac. Can you meet me in the Buck Rental Lot there?"

I hesitated before agreeing to meet him.

"What time does your flight get in?"

"I'm in now. How soon can you be out here?"

I looked at my watch. It was nearly midnight. I'd promised Tommy not to go out after dark.

"I can be out there in half an hour."

I hung up, grabbed my keys and headed for the car. I stopped, checked the door and found it wasn't locked, I pulled it open, and examined the door jamb. Then I looked at the door. Duct tape was covering the lock, keeping it from going into the door jamb. Who did that? How long had it been like that?

I ripped the tape off, as I phoned the police department. I asked for Tommy. He was on the streets. I left a message for him to meet me at the airport. The desk sergeant couldn't assure me when he'd get the message. He was tied up with a hostage situation on the other side of town. I told the desk sergeant to tell him it was urgent. I threw the phone down and raced out to the car. I opened the trunk and rummaged around for the Biretta and box of shells I'd stashed there. I finally found them under the spare tire. That wasn't where I'd left them. Then I remembered the kidnaping. They'd been in the car at the time of the kidnaping. I checked the gun. It looked as if it had been cleaned. I opened the box of shells. They looked fine. I threw a couple of handfuls of shells into my jacket pockets, and wished I'd remembered to buy another clip for it. One would have to do. I put one shell in the chamber, closed the slide, and popped the clip into place and put it in my purse.

I found myself speeding toward the airport, and then driving very slow, looking down side streets for a black and white. I didn't see one anywhere. I made it to the airport just as a plane was taking off. It swooped overhead as I entered the airport road. I drove around the parking areas, past the terminal and hesitated at the edge of the rental lot. I was blinded as someone in front of me flashed their brights in my eyes. I regained my eyesight in time to see a white Cadillac coming toward me. I slipped the gun into my purse, parked my car illegally at the side of the lot, and walked toward the car.

A man who reminded me of Gerry emerged from the car. He was the same height and the same weight and had the same eyes. I backed off as he held his hand out to me.

"Poppy?" he asked.

"Yes. You must be Harold Rivers. I'm glad to finally meet you."

"Come ahead and get in the car. I'd like to just drive around to talk. Don't want anyone eavesdropping on our conversation. Too much at stake here." He was trying to act frightened. I didn't quite buy it. How could you be that big, and be frightened of anything? I can't tell you why I did it, but I did as he said. Just as I was getting in the car, I heard someone call my name.

"Poppy? Is that you?"

I stepped back from the car and saw Prudy walking across the street.

"Prudy, where you heading?"

"Just coming to pick up my brother. He gets in on the 12:50 from Chicago."

"Tell him hello for me." I waved to her, and turned and got into the car. I saw her standing, staring at me, then she waved.

"Who was that?"

"Just a friend."

"I wish you hadn't drawn attention to us."

"What could it hurt. She's just a friend."

"Never mind." He put the car into gear and pulled out of the lot.  As we reached the end of the airport road we met the airport security car. I waved at the driver. I was surprised then, when instead of taking the road into town, Harold took the road that led to the country and the interstate.

"Why this direction.  Can't we stop at a restaurant and talk?"

"No."

I began to get nervous.  He wasn't being nearly as friendly as he'd been on the phone. I reached into my pocket and pushed my redial button, or I thought I did. I didn't hear anything. I took my hand out of my pocket.

He pulled onto the interstate and headed West.  I watched as the speedometer swept up to eighty and then to ninety.  As luck would have it, there were no state troopers patrolling this stretch of highway. In fact, it was deserted.  I found myself mentally identifying the trucks we met going East. I should have been thinking about what steps I was going to take to protect myself.  He still hadn't told me anything.

Just as I was beginning to think he wasn't going to say

a thing, he spoke.

"So, I suppose you want to know what could get Danny off?"

"That was the whole purpose of this excursion." I said.

"Well, Danny isn't guilty of murdering my brother. Do you know who is?"

"I thought I might have it figured out."

"I thought you might have it figured out, too."

"It isn't Gerry is it?"

"You're right."

He pulled into a rest area. It was deserted except for a Peterbilt tractor-trailer rig sitting across the drive. He pulled past the lighted area into a darkened spot under a tree. He lowered his window, and shut off the engine.

"Get out."

"The mosquitoes will eat us alive."

"Only one of us."

He was aiming a nickel-plated .357 Magnum Desert Eagle at me.

"Can you point that elsewhere, I'm allergic to nickel?"

"Can't you be serious about anything? I'm going to kill you."

"Why would you do that."

"You said you'd figured out who killed my brother."

"I could be wrong."

"Get out of the car." He waved the Magnum at me.

I still had the strap of my purse slung over my right shoulder. As I stepped out of the car, I slid my hand into my purse, wrapped my finger around the trigger and pointed the purse in his direction. The car was between us. I liked it that way.

"Get over here, now."

"I like the breeze on this side."

His face lit with rage as he stormed to my side of the car. I turned, keeping the gun aimed in his direction. A car pulled off the road and stopped under the lights. He turned toward it. It was my chance. I fired. Firing through a leather purse isn't entirely accurate. I missed. I pulled the gun out and let the purse fall next to the car.

He dodged behind the car and fired at me. I fled toward the picnic area, and he fired another shot at me, as I ducked behind a tree. Keeping score, that meant I had fifteen bullets left and he only had fourteen. Unless he had another clip in his pocket.

Several picnic tables were stacked at the back of the lot, I ran toward them. Another car entered the rest area. The next shot was muffled, as if the Magnum had been fitted with a silencer. It could have been quieter. I assumed he'd used it before. I pointed the gun in his general direction and pulled the trigger, and took off again toward the stacked picnic tables. I heard the silencer spit again, a little louder this time. I hit the dirt, and slid under an upright picnic table, rolled over and fired back. I think I killed a tree.

I held my breath. I'd lost him. He was too big to be hiding completely behind a tree. I concentrated on the silhouettes of each tree. One had a bulge at the spot where shoulders would be. I aimed at the bulge and fired. I heard a yelp of surprise. He stepped out from behind the tree and fired high. The silencer was losing its effectiveness. As he ran toward me, I fired once again, then turned and ran toward the stacked tables. I climbed behind them. How many shots do I have left? I didn't have time to remember. He fired three shots in succession at the picnic tables. Each shot sounded a little louder. I sat quietly. None of the shots had penetrated my barricade. From my left I heard a whisper.

"What you got there, a 9 mm.?"

I answered, "Yes." As I dove to the farther end of the barricade.

My previous position was peppered with holes. It had been a good time to move. I shrieked anyway. He'd fired three shots.

He stood and moved toward me. I turned and ran into a cornfield, pulling the trigger six times, waving the gun wildly behind me as I ran.     I was nearly twelve yards into the cornfield when I dropped down. It was more than knee high, and past the Fourth of July. Nearly chest high to me. He would have a harder time hiding in it.  I scrambled another twelve yards, then took advantage of a bare spot in the field, and scurried to the left a dozen rows.  I fell back and looked up at the stars, checked the tassels and found there was a slight breeze, and all of the tassels were rustling. It would give me a bit of cover, if I brushed the cornstalks as I moved. He would be looking for movement.  I found a fallen cornstalk loose on the ground, reached through the corn four rows over and bumped another cornstalk. The top of the cornstalk fell, as he fired at it. I crept quietly down the row toward a wooded area, nearly a quarter mile away.

I heard him crashing through the corn straight toward

me. I stood and fired four shots in his direction, and stood and ran toward the woods. He fired three shots at me, and came after me like a bull, screaming and raging.

"I've got you now. Your gun is empty." he shouted.

I ran until I reached the woods. I dove into a bramble bush, and scrambled further inside of it. I saw his legs as he rushed past me. I held my breath, and only began breathing as he charged further into the woods.

From the direction of the rest area, I heard someone calling my name. I didn't dare answer. I crept out of my hiding place, and dashed back into the cornfield, running until I heard Rivers shouting behind me. I ducked down into the corn, and began scrambling through the rows on my hands and knees, oblivious to whether or not I was shaking the cornstalks. As I got nearer to the rest area, I heard Tommy's voice calling my name. I stood up.

"I'm here, Tommy."

Just then a shot was fired from behind me. I spun around to return the fire, but another shot rang out from behind me, and I heard Rivers' cry out that he was hit.

I turned back to Tommy, ran toward him, and put my hands on my hips.

"Why did you do that!      I was going to do that.  It never fails.  I never get to shoot the bad guy, and I never get to change my own tire."  I complained.  Suddenly my knees grew weak, and I slumped to the ground.  I was shaking all over.  Tommy grabbed my hand, tilted my chin and looked into my eyes.  Then he stood and turned toward the cornfield.

Tommy cautiously approached the fallen man.  I struggled back to my feet and followed him.  Rivers was shot in the left shoulder.  As I approached, he was lying on the ground, moaning.  "I'm dying.  I'm dying.  Please help me."

"You're going to be all right.  Just lie still so I can get this bleeding stopped a little."  said Tommy.  As he ripped up Rivers' t-shirt to staunch the flow of blood, he simultaneously read him his rights.

"Gerald."  I said as everything suddenly clicked into place.

His eyes snapped open.  He looked more dangerous than helpless. He tried to sit, groaned and fell back.  "How did you know?" he asked.

"I didn't.  I just now figured it all out."

"What are you talking about?" asked Tommy.

"This isn't Harold Rivers.  This is Gerald Rivers, Gerry's

290

dad."

"I thought he was dead." Said Tommy.

"So did everyone else. This redheaded troublemaker spoiled the whole thing. You just couldn't keep out of it, could you?" said Gerald.

"There was something wrong. Every time I talked to you, my scalp tightened up. I couldn't put my finger on it. Then I remembered one of your neighbors saying, you were like two peas in a pod. I don't always pay attention, but the information goes in nevertheless. It just took a while for it to pop back out and make sense." I said.

"So who killed the other guy?" asked Tommy.

"Gerald here killed his brother, Harold." I said.

"Why didn't Gerry know his father was still alive?" asked Tommy.

"I suspect he did. You know the seriousness of Gerry's cocaine habit. I think Gerald here knew he could manipulate Gerry into doing anything for a steady supply."

"So why is Danny Johnson still in jail?" I whirled around feeling extremely guilty. I'd been caught. The speaker was Ralph.

291

## CHAPTER XXXXXI

I've always been able to track down Ralph, wherever he is. Ruth can't even find him like I can. I guess that's what makes me a good detective (don't tell anyone. Ralph thinks I'm a secretary or something). Anyhow, that's why I was so surprised to see Ralph standing behind me at the rest area. He can hardly ever find me when he wants me.

"How'd you get here?" I asked.

"I got a call from the police, telling me you were being kidnaped again by some guy in a white Cadillac. Then before I could get out of the house, I got another call saying you were being shot at here at this rest area." said Ralph.

"I didn't know you could drive that fast!"

"So have you figured out why Gerald Rivers killed his wife?" asked Tommy.

"I don't think Gerald did kill his wife. I think his brother

293

Harold killed her, and I think that's why Gerald killed Harold."

"This broad is way too smart. She's a danger to herself and society." This from Gerald. The EMS had arrived and were putting him on a stretcher. Their reassurances he wasn't dying, instead of being met with gratitude were met with greater hostility. Gerald was still alive, but he'd been found out.

"So why set up Danny to take the fall?" Ralph asked.

"I didn't. I don't know how that happened? I thought I killed Harold with my 30.06 rifle." said Gerald.

"I guess we better go get Danny out of jail. He's innocent!" I turned to Ralph. He just held his hands up in surrender.

## CHAPTER XXXXXII

It took us three more hours to get out of the cornfield and away from the rest area. Gerald was hauled away within half an hour. The Emergency Medical Technicians said he was doing so well, he'd need handcuffs as soon as he left the operating room! He didn't like the idea. I don't think he knew they were kidding. He would have a guard on his room, however.

It seems part of what Tommy couldn't tell me on our last date was Harold Rivers was not with the Drug Enforcement Agency in Washington, like he said. He was a major operator. As soon as Tommy learned Gerald survived and Harold hadn't, he got word to the people who needed to know. A lot of narcotics detectives sat up and noticed. It solved a lot of mysteries. It explained a lot of inconsistencies in Harold/Gerald's behavior. It cleared up a lot of puzzles.

Harold/Gerald's actions were no longer mysterious, they were as a result of a person not knowing what he was doing. Of course, Gerald didn't know half of the people involved, so when he tried to go back as Harold, he made a lot of people mad. He ignored important people on the street. There was a drug war starting between Harold's people and the major suppliers. Gerald was taking the money and keeping it. Probably partly out of greed and partly out of pure ignorance as to who got what.

By the time we got the prosecutor to hear Gerald's confession (which he later claimed was beaten out of him), and got to a judge for a release, it was nearly seven o'clock in the morning. The sun was just beginning to beat down by the time we got Danny released from jail.

We took Danny to Ralph's house. Ruth sent him into the bathroom for a shower, with a stack of Ralph's clean clothes. They were about the same size.

While Danny was in the shower, Tommy showed up. Ruth, looking wonderful for someone who had just climbed out of bed thirty minutes ago, fluttered around the kitchen, setting extra plates at the table, sending children to another bathroom to get ready for school, packing lunches, and fixing up a farmer's breakfast for her uninvited guests. Ralph likes efficient women.

When Danny came out looking relaxed and handsome I started. In Danny's case the man made the clothes...much sexier than Ralph in the same clothes. I'd have to tell Hazel with all of these good-looking, sexy guys around, it was much too early to choose just one.

Tommy told us he'd been piecing together information from his department and from the State Police.

"None of it made any sense. Harold was being followed and he didn't make the contacts we thought he would make. Important people on the other side tried to make contact with him, and he just blew them off. When we learned it was not Harold but Gerald, then it made sense. Gerald didn't know what he was doing!" explained Tommy.

"I've always felt guilty about Shorty dying in the mill. Do we know why Gerald killed him?" I asked.

"Gerald apparently thought Shorty recognized him. He thought you were on to him, as well. He claims he didn't think the bean bomb would cause much damage. The State Police arson investigation revealed a homemade detonator set off a small bomb in the office, and it caused a chain reaction explosion on the gases built up in the grain silos. The detonator was made with soybeans and water. When the beans swelled they were to set off a detonator. Gerald expected them to disappear entirely, or to be overlooked because the feed mill was full of soybeans. Unfortunately for Gerald, Poppy told the State Police she'd discovered some sprouted soybeans at the site as well as an army manual describing the detonator in Gerald's house. She turned it over to the State Police. It wasn't enough to convict Gerald. But it was enough to get a confession out of him. 'I might as well fry for two as for one.' were his exact words." explained Tommy.

The doorbell rang. Ruth had her hands full, and Ralph had children sitting on him, so I went to answer it. I was surprised to see a black Lexus sitting in the drive. The two people at the door introduced themselves. It was Victoria and her husband Alan, Danny's sister and brother-in-law.

"Sis. Al. What are you doing here?" asked Danny as I led them into the kitchen.

"Danny. I hate to tell you this, but your sisters have been causing a lot of grief for me." I told him.

"What have they done?"

"Well, they've been trying to protect you, as well as one

298

another, I think. Vicky here thought Evelyn killed Gerald. Alan thinks Vicky hired it done." I looked at them, and they tried to hide behind the refrigerator.

"I'm really sorry. I just didn't know what to think. I was afraid to come see you Danny. I thought Evelyn did it. I couldn't talk to Alan about it. He was terrified I'd hired someone to kill Gerald." said Vicky.

"I'm sorry Poppy. I guess we gave you a lot of scares. We didn't even talk about what we were doing. Vicky thought she was doing it to save Evelyn, and I thought I was doing it to save both of them. I thought they were either in it together or had hired someone. We didn't talk about it. We talked around it. So much for marital communication, I guess." said Alan.

"But why go so far as to put a bomb in my garage?" I asked.

"We didn't do that, Poppy." said Alan.

"So who did?" I asked.

"The profile was identical to that of a man who was last known to work for Harold's biggest competitor." said Tommy.

"Why would they want to hurt Poppy?" asked Ruth.

"Poppy knows everything." said Julia.

"Not nearly everything, child." I said.

299

No more than ten minutes after Vicky and Alan showed up, Evelyn and her husband showed up. They all took Danny (and Ralph's clothes) home with them. As they were pulling out of the drive, Town Marshal Everett Meadows from Fairview pulled in.

I let him into the house. He looked sheepish and apologetic.

"I should have known it wasn't Gerald that was killed. I worked with the man for five years. I should have known." he was very distraught. "I might as well resign. My powers of observation are really awful. I should have known it was him."

"Being town marshal doesn't usually require the detective skills that are necessary for the kinds of problems you've had to deal with. You've been swamped with more than a two-man police department that's short one man  can handle. Three murders in the past six months is quite a lot for such a small place. And then there's been all the assistance you've given the drug task force. You've done a fine job." Tommy reassured him.

"But why didn't anybody tell me that Harold and Gerald were twins?" I asked.

"I just thought everybody knew it. I thought I could tell

them apart. I guess I was wrong." Everett mumbled something about never being right.

Tommy rushed to discourage him from putting himself down. He changed the subject and asked if they'd found out anything more about the theft from the town clerk's office.

He told us the audit of the town records was completed and there had been receipts undeposited in the bank during the time Karen Arnold was in the hospital. They were unclear as to the identity of the thief, but three people had access to the money, Gerald, Karen, and Gerry. With Gerald still alive, Marshal Meadows believed he might find the answer.

"I suspect we'll find Gerald was the culprit." he said. His bravado had deflated severely. He apologized again. "I was acting like an asshole. I'm sorry ladies. I really didn't know how a town marshal was supposed to act, and Gerald was my only role model. I can't believe that he turned out to be the murderer. I feel so foolish. I should have known. After all, he killed Alice."

"But he didn't kill Alice. Harold killed Alice." I explained the circumstances.

"I should have known that, too. I should have known. How could I be so blind?" Nothing was going to convince

301

Meadows he wasn't inept, incompetent, and stupid.

"Oh, come on. You're being too hard on yourself."

"That's the least of it. You know I went back to the scene and went over everything again. There's no way, Gerald, 'er Harold could have been shot from the willow stand like I said. It had to have been from behind that dumpster over there. That's another thing, the dumpster. Nobody knows who ordered it. The State Police called the company that set it there, and got a name and billing address, but they're phony. I should have thought of all that. I'm so stupid. I should quit."

"You'll probably find that Gerald ordered it." Tommy went on. "In the meantime, you've been a great help to the drug task force, and the whole thing is about to bust loose. We just have one witness to bring in, and the whole drug network supplying this area should be crushed."

I looked at Tommy, worried.

He nodded, "Yeah, Gerry. He's volunteered to give us the information we need."

# CHAPTER XXXXXIII

Tommy brought me home, walked me to the door, and unlocked it. He checked under the beds and announced there was no one there except old boyfriends. I walked him back to the door, and he kissed me good night.

I promised to lock up good, and go to bed. I was still muddy from the cornfield. Ruth had helped me brush most of it off my clothes, but I still had it in my hair, and under my fingernails. I needed a long shower.

I had my clothes stripped off, and the water turned on when the phone rang. It was Gerry. I turned the water off, and grabbed it just as the answering machine picked up.

"Poppy. I have to talk to you."

"I'm here."

"I can't do this over the phone. Can I come over?"

303

"I have to take a shower. Give me half an hour."

"Sure."

Exactly one half hour later, the bell rang. Mousie ran to the door and paced back and forth as I walked toward it. I peeked out. It was Gerry. I opened the door, Gerry was dressed in black. Mousie rubbed up against him.

"I just heard about what happened. I'm sorry. I should have told you about Dad and Uncle Harold, but Dad was holding my drug addiction over my head."

"I'm really sorry, but why didn't you at least tell me he was still alive?" I asked.

"It was all so complicated. I didn't really find out about it all until after Dad killed Uncle Harold."

"Did you know it was really Gerald who'd killed Harold all along?"

"Not at first. I was too upset. But then we were at the funeral and Margaret Lafferty came up to me and hugged me, and then turned to Uncle Harold and said, 'Hello Gerald'. I thought Margaret had flipped out. But she was serious. I looked at him really good, and realized that it was really my Dad. He gave me a look that said, 'Keep your mouth shut." I just went straight home and moved out. He left town that night."

"While Dad was with Washington D.C. P.D. I got hooked on cocaine. Uncle Harold found out about it and threatened to tell Dad if I didn't help him out. He was running cocaine, one of the biggest dealers in D.C. I was supposed to make a big sale for Harold. I went crazy when I saw all that coke, and tried to cut myself in for a major portion of it."

I arched an eyebrow at him. He shook his head.

"It gets worse. Uncle Harold had to kill one of his guys to keep me from getting killed. Dad bungled into the middle of everything and Uncle Harold just barely got out of it before the whole thing went up. Three-quarters of his operation went to jail. His suppliers thought he'd turned them over to Dad out of spite or something. Anyhow, Mom was killed in retaliation, and then her brother was killed. I always figured they thought they were shooting Dad. That's why Dad quit the police department there and moved here."

"Why did your Dad kill Alice?"

"He didn't. Uncle Harold was here trying to get me to deal for him again. Alice walked in on it. She was talking on the portable phone with her daughter. Harold tried to make her think he was Dad. She knew it wasn't. She screamed at him

305

to keep his filthy drugs away from me.   She really did love me like I was her own son.  She started to pull a knife out  of the drawer, and told him she'd kill him if he didn't leave us all alone.  He shot her."

"How did he get your Dad to claim that he'd shot Alice?

"He threatened to turn me in as a drug dealer.  He had proof."

" And then your Dad killed your Uncle Harold and assumed his identity.  Why did he do that?"

"He really hated Uncle Harold for killing Alice.  Dad was upset because everyone was pointing at him, saying he got away with murder.  He wanted to make it look as if the mob had murdered Harold.   Then he changed his mind and assumed Harold's identity thinking he could get his hands on Harold's money that way.  Harold had a wife.  I only met her once.  They didn't live together.  Dad thought she'd get all of Harold's money."

"I can't figure out why he paid Ralph to defend Danny."

"I told him I'd turn him in unless he did.  I think he felt bad about Danny getting the blame for Harold's murder.  They weren't getting along so good when Harold murdered her, but I think Dad still loved Alice."

"Who changed the barrels on the rifles?"

"I did. Dad used my rifle to kill Harold. I did it before I knew Dad was still alive. I figured Uncle Harold was setting me up to take the fall. I couldn't go to jail. I was afraid there'd be no cocaine in jail. I hated seeing Danny there. He used to be my best friend. I still feel like he's my brother. But I just couldn't go to jail."

"I'm sorry I suspected you of killing your father, but you have to admit it was all pretty weird. I wish someone had told me earlier that Harold and Gerald were identical twins."

"I kept quiet because of the cocaine. I'd do almost anything for the cocaine." he admitted.

"I know. Why don't you quit?" I asked.

"I tried to. The other night... I knew you disapproved of me because of the coke. I tried to quit. I'd gone three days without it, trying to stay straight, so you'd like me. Then when I saw you with that cop, I just went crazy and started using again. I couldn't get enough."

"You said you weren't a druggie."

"Denial is the worst part."

"Get help."

"Do I have a chance with you if I do?"

307

"It's possible. Then again, you'd have a chance with a lot of nice girls. Nothing's impossible, Gerry."

"Well, I agreed to cooperate with the police and tell them everything I know about Uncle Harold's operation. Dad doesn't know much of anything. He couldn't hide from them. They would have gotten him sooner or later, while he was pretending he was Uncle Harold."

"That's a start."

"Then I guess I'm going to have to serve some time for stealing from the town clerk's office. That was me. I did it to pay for the coke."

"I know a good lawyer."

"If I try to clean myself up, do I have a chance with you, Poppy?"

"Don't say 'I'll try', say I will. You can do it. Just you see. Everything's going to be all right."

"I've got a feeling I'm going to have to hurry to be in the running with you, Poppy."

"Just remember nothing is impossible and change is good."

I showed him to the door, and said goodbye, just as the phone rang. It was Don. I waved at Gerry and closed the

308

door, took a deep breath and picked up the phone.

"Well, Hello there."

"You have a cute way of saying hello."

"Tell me you don't say that to all the girls."


The End

## EPILOGUE

I'll bet you're worrying about the box I kicked out into the garage. Well, let me tell you, the next day I remembered it, because Mousie kept going to the door and scratching. He sniffed. He growled. He snarled.

Finally, he said, "Haaarow. Haaaarwaaar-yow." That's what he always says. My friends say it sounds like he's saying, "Hello, how are you." It's highly possible. He keeps repeating the phrase over and over when he's excited about something. He said it the time someone stole the porch furniture. I thought he was talking to another cat. I swore then I'd always pay attention when he said it.

Reluctantly I got up and went to the door to the garage. I picked Mousie up, and he snuggled up next to me. As I pulled the door open, he struggled from my arms and ran to the box. He stalked around it, growling and snarling. I opened the overhead garage door, and kicked the box outside. Mousie ran back to me and put his front paws on my knees.

I'd just picked him up and turned to lower the garage door, when it happened.

But that's my next story. I hope you don't mind waiting.

THE END

A Teaser: AN EXCERPT from my next book, Don't Ask Twice due out sometime next year.

# DON'T ASK TWICE

### BY

### JANA LYNN SHELLMAN

CHAPTER ONE

I'm Poppy Hannah. I'm a paralegal and I usually work for Ralph Taylor, attorney at law. I've got these little psychic gifts, such as knowing who's on the phone when it rings, and knowing when a person is innocent. It doesn't extend to knowing who's guilty, and that's where I get in trouble. I can't stand to see an innocent person in jail, so I start doing a little snooping. I'm an amateur detective of sorts, and I spend a lot of time in and out of the office investigating to learn who's really guilty. Ralph gets upset about it. But he really gets upset when something dangerous happens.

As it turned out, they couldn't put the blame for the bomb on anyone. Someone was trying to kill me, but I figure he went straight to jail after a shoot out just after he put the bomb in the box. Last I checked, he was still there. At any rate, Ralph thought my safety was involved, so he loaned me to a college buddy, Joe Musica, an attorney in Huntington Beach, California. Joe had worked for the Orange County Public Defender's Office for years and wanted to finally go into private practice. He asked Ralph for help in organizing an office. Ralph thought he could keep me out of harm's way and help Joe at the same time. He sent me to California.

I'd heard Huntington Beach was wonderfully low in humidity, and the sunshine was constant year 'round. Humidity is my enemy. I have this ultra-curly red hair. When it rains I look like Bozo the clown. I agreed to go.

It was arranged I'd spend six months setting up Joe's office, hiring a legal secretary, and a paralegal, and training them in my efficient manner.

Joe picked me up at the airport in his 1979 Mercedes convertible. He was the most handsome man I'd ever seen in my life. He was wearing a polo shirt open at the neck. His skin was burnished a deep bronze. His hair was black and curly and fell over one eye. His eyes! His eyes were turquoise green, fringed in the blackest, thickest lashes I'd ever seen. His eyebrows were gorgeous. He was six foot four of well-sculpted, but not overstated muscle. I tried very hard not to stare at him. I certainly wouldn't have fought so hard and long with Ralph about the temporary change of climate, had I known the benefits included looking at Joe.

As he helped me into the car, I was pleased the top was down. Women everywhere were looking at me with envy...at least those who could tear their eyes away from Joe.

I'd asked Ralph what Joe looked like. He'd said, "Oh, just your average guy, I guess. A little taller than usual, but average." I'd have to tell Ralph's wife, Ruth, to have his vision checked.

This job was going to be harder than I thought. But a lot

more fun than I'd imagined. Joe drove me straight to the office he'd rented. It was a suite directly across the street from the beach. He showed me quickly through the office. It was vacant except for a beautiful hand-carved antique desk which sat in the largest room.

"That desk came from Italy by sailing ship in the 1800's." said Joe. "It belonged to my great-grandfather."

Pulling the drapes Joe showed me the view. Nothing but beach and ocean on two sides. As he directed me back through the adjoining room, he said, "This will be your office."

The view was almost as spectacular and would suit me fine. I cranked the window open, leaned out and took a deep breath. The scent was overwhelming, flowers were everywhere. It was much nicer than the view of the new parking garage I have in Ralph's office.

"This will do great, Joe." I glanced up from the window to find him staring at me, with what I perceived as admiration.

I convinced myself he was enjoying the flowers, the same as I.

As Joe ushered me out the office door he put his hand gently on my shoulder. I was hard put to name the feelings rushing over me, but would have to be practical and call them chemically induced. I sneaked a peak at Joe from time to time as he drove me to the door of the Waterfront Hilton in Huntington Beach. He jumped out of the car and beat the valet parking attendant to my door. He touched my shoulder once again as he helped me from the car. Once again I was assaulted by an overwhelming feeling leaving me speechless.

"You're to stay here, until we can find you an apartment or a house close to the office." He said. "You get changed, and I'll pick you up at 7:00 for dinner."

I was too flustered to speak, and nodded instead. My mind raced furiously in an attempt to get my mouth to work. As Joe pulled my carry-on bag from my hand and gave it to the bellman, he stooped and kissed my cheek.  Still in a state of confusion, I reached up and touched it, managed to say, "Goodbye." and turned toward the hotel.

The bell captain retrieved my bags from the Mercedes trunk and marched to the elevator.  I looked back to see Joe driving away, and quickly followed the bell captain to my room.

If I'd looked just to my right, I might have seen a man dressed in a tank top and bicycle shorts hiding in the bushes as I'd entered the hotel lobby.

Hope you'll look for the next

Poppy Hannah Mystery